FEB 12

A Hallie Marsh Mystery

San Francisco, Paris, New York, Washington, Santa Fe

Merla Zellerbach

Love to Die For

firefall^{tm}

First Edition: November 2011

cover design: BJR/EB

ISBN: 9780915090396

FIREFALL EDITIONS
Canyon California 94516-0189

literary@att.net
www.firefallmedia.com

Novels by Merla Zellerbach

LOVE TO DIE FOR
THE MISSING MOTHER
MYSTERY OF THE MERMAID
SECRETS IN TIME

Firefall Editions

RITTENHOUSE SQUARE

Random House

SUGAR
CAVETT MANOR
LOVE THE GIVER
THE WILDES OF NOB HILL

Ballantine

LOVE IN A DARK HOUSE

Doubleday

For Gary Zellerbach, the world's most loving son
and greatest jazz guitar player!

plus endless gratitude to my patient husband, Lee Munson, for
his suggestions and encouragement, to Linda, Laura and Randy
Zellerbach, my niece Brooke Kettner, and my mentor/publisher,
Elihu Blotnick.

Special thanks to Denise Marty of the Boom Model & Talent
Agency, to firefighters Alan Reynaud and paramedic/firefighter
Tiffany Woods & her spouse, my stepdaughter Anna Munson
Woods, to doctors Kevin Saitowitz, Robert Gilbert, Jerry Grodsky,
and my big brother, Sandor Burstein & his wife Beth.

I'm equally indebted to Phil Plant, Esq. & Barbara Schraeger, as
well as Judge Angela Bradstreet & Cherie Larsen for legal suggestions.

My stepchildren Gigi & Juan Monterrosa and Kathy & Eric Munson have been most supportive, as well as good friends Cissie Swig,
Sharon Litsky & John Sampson, Sen. Dianne & Dick Blum,
Gretchen de Baubigny and Anne & Roger Walther, Ellen & Wal-
ter Newman, and Helen Hilton Raiser.

Hollywood scribe George Christy has been wonderfully inspiring,
and Pat Dodson had some great ideas on how to get away with
murder.

LOVE TO DIE FOR

PART 1

— Chapter 1 —

**Mid-morning
December 1st, 2010**

THE SHATTERING SOUND of crashing cars made Hallie Marsh drop her groceries and rush towards the intersection. Screaming, "Call 911!" to a passerby, she ran to the collision site. A silver Infiniti heading east had plowed into the side of a blue BMW heading south.

Pounding on his door, the Infiniti driver was trying frantically to escape the steaming car. His airbag had imploded, his pale face showed shock, but he seemed unhurt. Hallie grabbed the handle and the door opened instantly. The man mumbled a weak, "Thank you," climbed out, took a step, and dropped to the ground.

"Oh, God," Hallie groaned. She fell to her knees, shook his shoulders briefly, then searched his neck for a pulse. There was none.

Recalling the recent CPR course she'd taken with her fiancé, Cas, she knew that every second counted. Finding the notch at the tip of his breastbone, she placed one hand over the other, and began pushing hard and fast. Each compression went deep, and she remembered to release her hold for an instant before continuing.

After five or so minutes, she heard what sounded like a gasp, and again felt for a pulse. Miracle of miracles, there was one. He was breathing.

"Quick!" she said. "We need to turn him to keep his airway open." A pair of teenage boys who'd gathered to watch, bent to help. Once they had the man propped on his side, he began to show signs of life. His head moved slightly, his cheeks were regaining color, his breathing was almost audible. He blinked, opened his eyes and asked a silent question.

"You're going to make it, my friend," Hallie whispered, as the shrieking sirens drew near.

— Chapter 2 —
Noon the Same Day

TEN HANDSOME BACHELORS in flower-patterned swim trunks stood side by side on the stage, and Edith Marsh told her daughter she could have any one of them.

Hallie stiffened in her chair. "You're being ridiculous, Mother. I'm getting married in two months, in case you forgot. Why do you keep trying to fix me up?"

"Because I haven't booked the hotel yet. There's still time to change your mind and wait a few more years till you're sure."

"I am sure. Please make the wedding arrangements or we'll elope."

With a sigh, Hallie leaned back and stared at the program. The Bachelor Auction in the Fairmont Hotel on Nob Hill benefited one of her mother's favorite charities, Compassion & Choices.

And while Hallie strongly supported having end-of-life options, her mind was focused on the man whose life she'd help save a few hours earlier. The paramedics had praised her effusively as they lifted him on a stretcher. A police officer had taken her name and informed her that the other driver had died on impact. Witnesses reported the BMW had illegally zoomed through a red light, while the Infiniti had crossed the intersection on the green. The survivor was a well-known local Judge named Paul Dodson.

"Bachelor number seven is quite handsome," said Edith, unaware her daughter's thoughts were elsewhere. "The Fronds are good friends from an old San Francisco family. Don't you think he's handsome?"

"No. I don't."

Accustomed as Hallie was to having her domineering-but-loving mother try to run her life, she couldn't help but resent her attitude at a time when she should be sharing her daughter's happiness. Her future son-in-law, Daniel James "Cas" Casserly, was not only better-looking than any of the men on stage, he was smarter, funnier, sweeter, kinder, and sexier, for sure. He also had too much pride to allow himself to be "sold" to the highest bidder – even for a great cause.

Bidding was becoming competitive.

"Six hundred," announced the auctioneer, "six hundred going once. Do I hear seven hundred?"

"One thousand!" shouted Edith.

"One thousand it is! Do I hear eleven hundred?"

Hallie slid down in her seat, praying none of her friends in the press would see her.

"One thousand going once…your last chance, girls, for an exciting date with bachelor number seven. Do I hear eleven hundred? Going once, going twice — sold for one thousand dollars to the lady in the red hat!"

He banged his gavel, everyone clapped, and Hallie moaned.

— Chapter 3 —
Later That Afternoon

THE SPARSELY-FURNISHED ENTRANCE to the public relations firm, Hallie Marsh Communications, Inc., was a study in minimalism, and a tribute to one of the owner's idols, the late architect Mies van der Rohe. His famous phrase "Less is more" suited Hallie, not only in décor, but in the way she dressed, worked and lived. Simplicity, and an absence of frills and clutter were words she not only preached, but practiced with a passion.

Or as Cas once observed, some of her favorite expressions were "Bottom line," "End of discussion," and "Let it go." Patience was not one of her assets.

Yet underneath the pretty-blonde exterior dwelt a creative and practical publicist, a complex woman with compassion and a heart of gold — or stone — depending on the situation. She had taught herself to be tough when she had to be, and although it went against her gentler instincts, she was, above all, a survivor.

Earlier in the year, having proven to herself that she could build and run a successful business, Hallie had begun taking nonprofits as clients, spending half her time helping charities and groups in need, either pro bono or at a fraction of her usual charge. The jobless and the homeless were never far from her mind.

"How was your lunch? Did Mumsy buy you a nice bachelor boy toy?"

Hallie scooted past her assistant/receptionist and

sometimes-chauffeur Ken Skurman, pausing briefly to tug his ponytail. "Bug off."

"Ouch! Is he divinely handsome?"

"To die over," she called from her office.

"If you don't want him, send him to me?"

No answer, he knew, meant that she was opening her snail mail, reading her email or listening to voicemail.

— Chapter 4 —

IN TRUTH, HALLIE was trying to do all three. Multitasking, as she once explained to Ken, didn't really mean focusing on two or three things at once. It meant a series of focusing first on one item, then another, then possibly a third, then going back to the first, etc. — without giving each too much attention.

(Ken had disagreed, pointing out that he could brush his teeth and pee at the same time, thus ending the discussion.)

Tossing a letter into the recycling basket under the desk, Hallie glanced about her office, smiling to herself as she remembered Cas's first visit to the all-white room. He was already in love with her, so his reaction didn't much matter, but his eyes had widened in disbelief as he'd stared around him.

The walls were blank, except for a single Dali watercolor. Roman shades dressed up a window overlooking historic Market Street. No bookcases, pictures, or shelves of knick-knacks were visible, only a pair of tall file cases, a stunning Lucite desk, two stark Lucite chairs that signaled,

"Don't get too comfortable," and a coat rack.

Unlike Cas's own work surface, piled high with electronic equipment and papers, Hallie's desk top was limited to essentials: her 20-inch computer screen, a printer/fax/copier, a white phone and speakers, and several neat stacks of folders.

She and Cas had met two years prior, on a luxury cruise ship. Edith Marsh had bought the trip for her daughter and a girlfriend right after Hallie's double mastectomy. The cancer hadn't spread, and luckily, disappeared along with her left breast. Removal of the right one had been a preventive measure.

Tall and slim, with dark hair, prematurely gray sideburns, and horn-rimmed glasses perched on a well-shaped nose, Cas was a much-awarded author, magazine editor, and journalist, traveling aboard the ship as a guest lecturer. Once he'd spotted Hallie, he had courted her relentlessly. She had feared her "boob-less-ness," as she called it, would turn him off, but it hadn't bothered him in the slightest. He admired her sharp brain and her independence, and they fell in love.

Edith Marsh had been shocked to hear her daughter come home from a six-week cruise talking of marriage. It seemed obvious that the two had only known each other in the most romantic and unrealistic of circumstances. Cas was good-looking, Edith admitted, but his membership in AA branded him as undesirable husband material. And did he know she had no breasts? Yes, she'd answered with a straight face. No need to explain they'd shared a cabin for the last week of their cruise.

Unable to talk the couple out of getting married, Edith had offered a bribe. She would host their wedding and buy them a house if they would live apart — and presumably date others — for two years.

Hallie said, "No way," but Cas said, "Way!" He told her he could never afford a big wedding or a multi-million dollar home, and they could still be together for two years even if they didn't share the same address. Not wanting a family rift, Hallie gave in, took a separate apartment to please Mumsy, and spent all her nights with Cas. Happily, the two years would be up in January.

Chapter 5

THE EARLY MORNING *Chronicle* gave Hallie a shock. Staring back at her from the front page was her own picture and not a very good one. It showed her in profile, on her knees giving CPR, hair flying in the wind. The photo was probably snapped by an onlooker's cell phone.

"SOCIALITE RESCUES JUDGE FROM CAR CRASH" was the eye-grabber, and much as she hated the S-word, she knew that it drew attention. A subtitle in smaller print read: "Marsh heiress rushes to aid Judge Paul Dodson."

The article reported:

"Helen-Louise 'Hallie' Marsh, 34, daughter of philanthropist Edith Marsh and the late R. Stuart Marsh, renowned art collector and onetime curator of the de Young Museum, is credited with saving the life of Superior Court

Judge Paul Dodson. Marsh was walking home from Cal-Mart grocery in Laurel Village, when the car crash occurred yesterday, at 10:14 a.m., at the intersection of California and Laurel Streets.

"According to witnesses, Marsh dashed to the scene and helped Dodson from his car. When he fainted, she administered CPR until the ambulance arrived."

Not true, Hallie thought. He'd already come back to life. But she read on:

"Dodson, 66, is in stable condition at San Francisco General Hospital. His wife, Dagmar Dodson, made a brief statement: 'Paul has heart complications, but I'm told he'll recover. He's in good spirits and we're all extremely grateful to Ms. Marsh for her heroic rescue.'"

"Good Lord!" she whispered. Reading on, Hallie learned that the other driver was a restaurant owner from Southern California. He had an open bottle of beer in the car and a blood-alcohol level at .10 percent. At the time of the collision, he was .02 percent over the legal qualification for inebriation. And she was, suddenly, in the local spotlight.

Chapter 6

THE REST OF THE DAY, the phone rang non-stop, emails poured in to her office, and a giant orchid plant arrived. The gift card, signed "Paul," included a scribbled "Thanks, I owe you a big one," and a cell phone number. Somewhat dazed by the attention, she signaled her assistant, Ken, to take all calls. Then she shut down her computer and closed the door, indicating she was not to be disturbed.

Her brain was wrestling with conflicting emotions. Yes, there was joy and pride at being celebrated, but there was also guilt. It wasn't a "heroic rescue" in the true sense. She didn't risk her life to save the man from drowning or burning or gunfire, and he probably would have survived without her.

Cas had said she did the right thing; he was proud of her. Mumsy, however, had issued a warning: "Don't ever be a good Samaritan! Once these people find out you have money, they'll think up all sorts of reasons to sue you or get a settlement."

Well, poof, she thought. You don't think of money when someone's in trouble. And it wasn't her fault she was born into a prominent family. All the more reason to help someone in trouble.

And yet, she told herself, even if she didn't deserve the accolades, and even if the guy hadn't been a Judge and she hadn't been a "socialite," she still deserved credit for trying to help. Maybe she did save his life. Who knows?

It struck her as ironic, too, that after years of struggling to get her clients' name in the papers, she'd inadvertently managed to get her own name — and picture, no less — on the front page. But instead of sweating it, she reminded herself of her mantra, "Let it go." And taking it all in perspective, she was able to do just that.

— Chapter 7 —

THE FOLLOWING MONDAY, a typical foggy San Francisco

16

morning, Hallie awoke early, tiptoed out of Cas's bedroom and drove to her apartment in Presidio Heights, a prime residential area. There she showered, washed her long blonde hair, fluffed it with a hair dryer and tied it back with a black ribbon. Almost automatically, she slipped into a beige pantsuit, added light makeup — and again, she was off.

Arriving at the office before Ken, she picked up a ringing phone. "Hallie Marsh Communications. Good morning."

"Hallie? I'm Egan Frond, the bachelor you bought," came a pleasant voice. "I'm calling to collect my date."

She took a few seconds to remember. "Oh — yes, of course. My mother bought you for me as a gift. But I have to tell you right off — I'm engaged to be married."

"Wonderful — congratulations!" He sounded relieved. "I'm not exactly free, either, but that's confidential. By the way, I saw your picture in the paper. You're quite a hero. May I at least take you to lunch?"

She started to regret the invitation, then realized her mother would ask questions. "Thanks, that would be lovely. Would Thursday work? Perhaps downtown?"

"The Rotunda at Neiman-Marcus has great popovers."

"Meet you there Thursday at noon," she said. "Wear swim shorts so I'll know you."

— Chapter 8 —

EGAN FROND WAS WAITING at the entrance when Hallie

17

arrived, prompt as always. She recognized him immediately. "You even look good with your clothes on," she teased, in a louder-than-normal voice.

He smiled and kissed her cheek. "So do you, sweetie. This kind gentleman will lead us to our booth."

What a surprise! He had a sense of humor and lunch would be less deadly than expected. No sooner had they sat down than a waiter appeared. "May I get you something to drink?"

"Hetch-Hetchy water, please."

"Sorry, Ma'am, we only have Evian and Perrier."

Egan held his laughter. As almost everyone but the young waiter knew, Hetch-Hetchy was the reservoir that supplied the city's tap water. "In that case," he said, "just fill a glass from the faucet."

Rolling his eyes, he turned to Hallie. "Thanks for coming today. You're a beautiful woman. I hope your fiancé doesn't mind."

"Hardly. He has dozens of females hunkering after him. Besides, he hasn't time to be jealous. But thanks for the compliment."

Despite Cas's disdain for men who paraded half-nude for charity, she found herself liking her new companion. He was shorter than she remembered, casually dressed in a navy hoodie and khakis, and sported the trendy "designer stubble" that men under fifty seemed to think attractive.

"He's a lucky guy."

"And so is your —" Instinct made her pause. "Girl-friend?"

"You're very perceptive." He lowered his voice. "It's not a 'she.' But my parents can't accept that I'm gay. Mom's coming around, but Dad says it's a perversion, and that if I ever come out of the closet, he'll disown me."

"That's terrible!"

He shrugged. "I love my Dad but he's a major pain in the butt. He doesn't get it. Doesn't get anything! The good news is that I'll be thirty-five in June. Then I can access my trust fund, and I won't need his bleeping money."

"But between now and then —"

"Yes, I have to lay low, so to speak. One day you'll meet my partner. He's a brilliant artist. But first things first. Tell me about you."

"After we order?"

"Fair enough," he laughed. They each chose a Crab Louis, then Hallie said, "My background's not too thrilling. I was born here, got a master's in education from Smith College, and expected to teach deaf children. The rest is even more boring."

"Please go on?"

"Okay. While I was job-hunting, I did some charity work publicizing events, and amazingly, that led to an offer to join a PR firm in New York. After six years in Manhattan, I came home and opened my own PR firm. The recession isn't helping, but we're still in the black. What about you, Egan? Don't you manage a winery?"

"Not so fast! I Googled you so I know that your father died in 1998, and your mother has a fabulous art collection. I know that you saved a judge's life a week ago, and you've a brother who lives in Southern California —"

She nodded. "Robbie did live there. He told us that's the place to be if you want to make it in the music world. What he really wanted was to get away from mother, who's a wee bit domineering. That's like saying Einstein was a wee bit smart. Anyway, now that he's 32, he figures he can handle her and he's moved back home. He's a jazz guitarist — really cool."

"I play the flute. I'm cool, too."

"Are you a flautist or a flutist?"

"I'm a flute player. Can I meet your brother sometime?"

"Absolutely!" The waiter brought hot popovers and soon after, they were munching their salads and chatting like longtime friends.

PART 2

— Chapter 9 —

Thursday, December 9th

"THE BOOBS, DARRYL, show me the boobs!"

Tall, slim, and strikingly beautiful, Darryl Woods leaned over the yacht railing and struck a pose.

"Yes, that's it — pensive, thoughtful. You're looking towards the bridge, but you're a million miles away. Soft, dreamy. Chin up a bit. That's it! Terrific! I like it!" Click! Click! Click!

The photographer knew he had to snap fast before the look became frozen. That meant taking dozens of shots of the same pose. Somewhere in the batch, he'd find a winner.

"Just a few minutes more, Darryl," he said. "I know you're tired. We all are. It's been a long morning. Put the hat back on — yes, tilt it — no, keep the brim up. Let's show off the swim suit. Yes, profile is good. Tummy in, tits out. Relax." Click! Click! Click! "OK, girls, we're done for today. Thanks for your patience. We'll be in touch."

Darryl waved goodbye, grabbed her terry cloth robe and hurried to the dressing room. Swim suit shoots were hard; every teeny bit of fat or bodily imperfection showed. Neither problem, however, worried her at the moment. A cram diet had helped, but after three days of having eaten next to nothing, she was ravenous.

Fortunately, she was one of the few models who had full breasts and enough cleavage to be of interest. Photographers often singled her out for that reason. And their shoots paid well. It was worth a few days of starvation.

Dressed and back in her car, she left Yacht Harbor in the Marina, and headed towards a designer's studio in downtown San Francisco. Makeup from the shoot was heavy, and made her skin itch, but she had one more date to keep before she could wash it off.

Glancing in the car mirror, she decided no repair work was needed. Her long, black hair had been carefully combed, and she liked what the stylist had done. Flat at the top, parted in the middle, it fell to her shoulders and below, silky and straight, cupping her face and lovely, chiseled features. Large blue eyes, shadowed and underlined, stood out against pale pink skin. The makeup artist had penciled her lips, carefully shaping them, then filling in with Schiaparelli-pink lip gloss. A glorious palette.

— Chapter 10 —

THE FASHION SHOW REHEARSAL took longer than expected. Designers liked to teach the models how to walk — it was their personal trademark. This designer left no doubts as to what she wanted: "Head forward, lean slightly back, shoulders relaxed, butt tight. Walk fast, crossing your feet in front of each other, and pretend you're stomping out a spider with each step. Do *not* smile; look bored and above it all."

Darryl learned the new step quickly, and took time to exchange her uplift bra for a breast-flattening camisole, although she couldn't completely hide her assets. After trying on a dozen outfits, she was given six to model. Then she was fitted for stiletto pumps, told to practice her walk, and to arrive three hours before the show for hair, makeup and accessories. The glamorous life of a model — some glamour, she thought wistfully. Life is so ironic.

Her watch said ten to four, and she hadn't eaten since breakfast. The nearest available food source was Eunice's Cafe, a small sandwich shop on Sacramento Street. To her delight, a car pulled out of a parking place a few doors down; she drove right in.

The Cafe was tiny, with a counter on one side. Directly opposite, a lone woman sat at one of two tables, nibbling a roll and staring at her iPad.

"Tuna on whole wheat, hold the mayo," Darryl told the man behind the counter. "Ooh — and a bowl of that hot lentil soup."

"Coming up!" He scribbled her order, handed it to a helper, and looked quizzically at his customer. "You've come here before. Are you a movie star or something?"

Darryl laughed. "No, I'm a poor, starving model. Could I please have that soup?"

"Sure thing." He dipped his ladle into a large pot and handed her a steaming bowl. "Careful. It's hot."

"Thanks." She carried her precious cargo to a table just as the door opened and a young man entered. He wore Levis, a blue shirt, and a leather jacket slung over his shoulder. Obviously in a hurry, he ordered a ham and cheese to go, turned around, spotted Darryl and did a double-take. Then he approached her. "Pardon me for staring, but you remind me so much of my sister, Hallie Marsh. Could you possibly know her?"

"Nope." Darryl set down her spoon and looked up pleasantly. She'd heard that line — and all its variations — before.

"Then please excuse me. I didn't mean to disturb you."

Nodding, Darryl returned to her soup, trying hard not to gobble it down and scorch her tongue. The young man turned his back and took a stool at the counter.

Had she been rude? Had she shown her impatience at being interrupted during her feeding frenzy? The man had been polite, and now that she'd taken a minute to notice, was not unattractive. About six foot two, she guessed, with a lean frame, and blond hair that needed trimming. He looked to be in his early thirties.

"Ummm - sir?" she said quietly.

He looked over. His face was angular with handsome all-American features. Freckles covered a straight, slightly turned-up nose. Light-colored brows hovered over intense brown eyes, now staring at her questioningly.

"I'm sorry," she said. "I didn't mean to be rude. If you'd care to sit in a chair, please join me."

"Thank you, I wish I could. I'm Rob — Rob Marsh. I grew up here, moved to Santa Monica — that was a mistake, so now I've moved back. My Mom's having a Christmas party, and I'm rushing home to change. She wouldn't appreciate my showing up in jeans."

"Can't blame her." What an intense young man! Well, what the hell. "I'm Darryl Woods. I've just come from work and I'm famished, so forgive me while I dig into my soup."

"Dig away." He reached into his pocket. "Here's my card. I'm a jazz guitarist and my band is really hot if you ever need music."

"I'll remember that." She smiled and tucked the card in her purse.

"Well — goodbye." He picked up his sandwich at the counter, then spun around. "Hey, would you like to hear me play tonight?" Before she could answer, he scribbled a time and address on the back of another card and set it by her soup bowl. "No need to RSVP. I'll put you on the guest list."

Then he hurried out the door.

— Chapter 11 —
That Evening

EDITH MARSH LIVED in a grand mansion on outer Broadway, San Francisco's "Gold Coast." Originally designed by famed architect Willis Polk, the awesome Georgian manor with its four stories of red brick respectability, was built in 1920 at a cost of $40,000. Edith and her husband bought it for $3.7 million in 1978. At the height of the dot-com explosion in the late 1900's, she turned down an unsolicited offer of $12 million. Her home was not for sale at any price.

Spanning two lots, the structure had views in almost every room, including the three-car garage and English Garden. An indoor swimming pool boasted a retractable ceiling for rare sunny days.

Edith Marsh's 300-guest reception had started out to be a small Welcome Home party for her son. Rob Marsh, however, had wanted no part of "being on display for your snooty, artsy-fartsy friends." Edith had persisted, and Rob, equally stubborn, threatened not to appear. Neither would budge until Hallie offered a compromise. It would be a Christmas party. Rob and his swinging jazz band would play by the pool. That way he could get his group known, his buddies would earn a few bucks, and he wouldn't have to be "Edith's prodigal son" who finally came home. Mumsy could point him out if she wanted to, but he'd be too busy to mingle.

A small army of California Parking valets stood lined up at the curb, awaiting guests. They came en masse — men in ties and dark suits, older women in black dresses and furs or stylish tops and pants, younger men and women in just about everything. All entrusted their BMWs, Bentleys, Bugattis, and an occasional Jaguar to the blue-jacketed valets. Several limos pulled up, deposited their passengers, and found a place on the street. The drivers would soon convene, have a smoke or two, exchange gossip and wait out the party.

At the front door, a hefty six-foot-four security guard stood watch, while a good-looking blonde in black checked off each guest. Just beyond, in the entrance hall, another line of tuxedo-clad waiters held trays with glasses of wine, champagne, and Perrier. Any reasonable beverage was available.

Darryl Woods, relieved to find her name on the list, followed the new arrivals down a long hallway to the living room. Intent on taking it all in, she noticed the people, the art, the decor. It seemed every available space was filled with a treasured vase, sculpture, or collection of art objects. She wondered if some had to be moved to make room for celebrity-florist Stanlee Gatti's massive flower arrangements.

Antiques were not Darryl's area of interest, yet she could see that the lavish furnishings were chosen with great care and taste, not to mention money. The décor reminded her of a concept she'd learned in an art course: "horreur de vacui" — fear of the void. Some people had a need to fill every possible space.

Yet the house was fascinating to see, and most likely she'd never have another chance. During her twelve-year marriage to corporate executive Wellman Swift, she'd been a guest in many upscale homes, but none quite as extravagant.

A waiter touched her arm. "May I get you a drink?"

"No, thanks," she said. "I'm looking for Mr. Marsh — Rob Marsh?"

"Yes, indeed. You'll find Mr. Marsh and his quartet at the swimming pool. Go right at the tulips, down the stairs and follow the noise — er, music."

She nodded a thank-you, dismissing a momentary temptation to turn around and escape. In the year since her divorce, she'd learned that it wasn't easy attending events alone. People, particularly those in the upper social strata, were not friendly, and made little effort to meet someone new. You could stand alone for half an hour before anyone would talk to you or invite you to join their group.

Still, she'd heard of Edith Marsh and her philanthropic credits, and she'd found Rob Marsh's invitation to his mother's mansion irresistible. She wondered how old he was, if he had a girlfriend, or if he was — like one musician she knew — married to his guitar. She hoped not. Rob's warmth and spontaneity were refreshing.

PART 3

— Chapter 12 —

HEADING toward the music, Darryl found herself in a large roofed-in courtyard. Fresh carnations wound around tall marble columns, waiters passed trays of hot hors d'oeuvres, and at a small table, Grimaldi, the Marsh butler, offered toasted rounds topped with caviar. A band of casually dressed musicians seemed almost out of place playing Duke Ellington and Cole Porter songs by the side of an oblong pool. Groups of lilies floated in the water, reflecting the priceless Monet on the wall. Too much, she thought. Sensual overkill.

She spotted Rob immediately. His head was bowed, nodding to the beat; he was lost in another world. His fellow musicians were equally focused on their drums, tenor sax, and stand-up bass, seemingly unaware of the crowd enjoying them.

"Hello," said a friendly voice.

Darryl turned to see an attractive young woman with long blonde hair.

"I'm Hallie Marsh. I grew up here." She smiled. "I saw you looking at my brother. Are you a friend of Robbie's?"

"Well, yes and no." Darryl introduced herself and told of their brief meeting. "I'm flattered that he thought I reminded him of you. But I really don't know Rob at all — Robbie?"

"He prefers Rob."

"He seemed so nice, so enthusiastic. And I admit I was curious about this house."

"Good for you, Darryl! He's a good-looking guy and you're — single? I'd have done the same thing."

31

"I've been divorced for a year. The scars take time to heal."

"I know." Hallie nodded. "I was married at nineteen for four months. But let me show you around and have you meet some friends." They chatted as they started to walk. "You mentioned you met Rob after a modeling job. Where do you work?"

"I'm with the Zoom Model & Talent Agency. I go wherever they book me. I work pro bono for charities, too. As long as I do it on my own time, the agency —"

"Hey, look who's here!" Rob's excited voice broke into their conversation. Carefully setting down his guitar, he yelled, "Guys, we're taking a break!" and hurried towards the object of his excitement, who was about to disappear in the doorway. To Darryl's surprise, he came up and kissed her cheek. "I can't believe you're actually here," he exclaimed. "I just looked over and saw the most beautiful woman in the world!"

"You mean women, don't you?" teased Hallie.

"Sisters don't count." He took Darryl's arm. "Can we go somewhere and talk for a few minutes? Nothing personal, Hal, but get lost."

"What about your band?"

"We're due for a break."

Hallie laughed. "Nice to meet you, Darryl."

— Chapter 13 —

BEFORE HE PLAYED HIS LAST SET, Rob asked Hallie to see that Darryl met some guests ("but no single guys!"), until

32

he could safely get away.

In order to do so, he'd had to allow his mother to introduce him and his band. He'd kissed, hugged, and publicly thanked her, sent his fellow musicians home, then by prearrangement, met Darryl at Osteria, a small Italian restaurant.

Although close in distance, it was warm and casual, and worlds away from the formal Marsh mansion. Despite having snacked at the party, both were hungry.

"I want to know every little thing about you, good or bad," he said, after they'd ordered their pasta. "Where'd you grow up?"

'I'm not sure I did," she smiled. "But I was born in the East Bay, went to Piedmont High and studied acting. The summer after graduation, I got involved with a small theater group here in the city. A man who saw me in a play asked me out. I married him at eighteen and never got to college."

"You're married?"

"Not now, thank goodness. He was sixteen years older, a corporate guy, and my self-appointed mentor. I lasted for twelve years before I got tired of being a trophy wife and wanted a life of my own. Fortunately, the Judge was a woman, and made him pay my legal fees."

He reached across the table for her hand. "What a jerk your husband was — to lose you."

She placed her hand on his for a few seconds, then drew gently away. "Now it's your turn to talk, Rob."

"Not yet. Are your parents alive? Do you have siblings?"

33

"No. My wonderful Mom died five years ago. Dad owned a chain of discount stores. He never made much money until he sold the stores in 2006, just before the recession. Then he married Brenda, a woman who'd worked for him. I'm pretty sure she married him for his money and she's doing her best to spend it so he won't leave it to me. But she's good to him, and he needs her."

"So — modeling pays your rent?"

She nodded. "Pretty much. Dad sends me checks when she's not looking."

"Care for cheese?" The waiter set down two plates of pasta. He disappeared and returned a moment later with a chunk of parmesan and a grater.

"How can you eat all that pasta and model bathing suits?" asked Rob. "Don't get me wrong. I love to see a woman enjoy her food."

"I'm through with bathing suits for now, so I can eat again. Starving myself beats taking furries."

"Furries?"

"I shouldn't tell you, it's an industry secret. But some models take a pill called furosemide — generic Lasix. It's a diuretic. They, um — get rid of all their water and look very thin."

"Sounds awful."

"Photographers hate it because the girls have to keep interrupting the shoot to run to the bathroom."

He shook his head in wonderment. "I guess it's my turn to talk now. What do you want to know?"

"What was it like growing up in that mansion?"

"I grew up in a much smaller house, Darryl. The

mansion came after Dad died and Mom wanted a big place to show off all her junk."

"Junk?" She speared a gnocci. "Mmm — heavenly."

"I guess junk's not a good word. Sorry you didn't meet Mom at the party. She can be charming, and people like her, but you see, she's owned by her possessions. I realize it's not too shabby to be owned by Picassos and Monets and Cézannes, but Mumsy — we call her that because she's so not a Mumsy – will always be the queen of control freaks. I love her, but she treated me like one of her paintings, which is why I moved away. Now that I'm back, she's trying hard to let me live my own life."

"You're a talented guitarist. Isn't she proud of you?"

"She thinks it's a nice hobby. She'd like me to be the curator of her art works. I keep telling her that music is my life, not art." He sighed. "For my thirteenth birthday, my Dad bought me a guitar and some lessons. I took to it right away, and in a few years, I was playing in small blues and rock bands around town."

"I went back east to Brandeis University," he continued, "and formed a progressive jazz-fusion group with some of my classmates. Then a high school buddy who lived in L.A. invited me to join his band in Hollywood. That went nowhere."

He grinned and picked up his fork. "The long and short of it is that I was broke. I came home, swallowed my pride, borrowed money from Mom and opened an art gallery selling holograms — three dimensional photographic images. I did okay, but Mom thought they were schlock, so I sold the gallery, and you know the rest."

35

"Yes, you're your own man at age — ?"

"Thirty two. Fair is fair, lovely lady. And you're about — twenty-six?"

"Right on! I'm twenty-six when I'm on a modeling job. And even at that age, I'm over the hill. For a high fashion shoot, they want eighteen-year-olds, and gals up to their mid-twenties."

"And when you're not modeling?"

"Thirty-one, but not for publication or I'll be answering the calls for 'an older woman.' "

He laughed. "I don't think so. Why do you work so hard?"

"Good question. When I was younger, I wanted to be a supermodel. I used to read Cindy Crawford's and all the famous girls' bios and how they got to where they are. It's competitive and it's vicious, and yet every model's ambition is to work for Victoria's Secret. They're like a family, though, and it's almost impossible to break in. After that, it's the *Sports Illustrated* swim suit issue. The big prize is to get on the cover. Or to get a makeup or fragrance campaign and make a hundred thousand dollars."

She paused to shrug. "But those were childhood dreams. At thirty-one, I think I need a new career — maybe in fashion design. Or maybe working for a non-profit that teaches students to use patterns and make clothes. I may even go back to school."

"In the meantime, you're getting well-paid?"

"Yes, especially when I do ads for Macy's and Bloomingdale's. If you know a photographer, he or she can recommend you for jobs, and that's a big plus. You can make a thousand a day on a good shoot. Some jerks will try to get you to pose free. They'll say, 'You need these pix in your portfolio. We won't charge you and we'll spread them around.' That's pure BS. No good model poses free, except for charity."

"It's today's world, I'm afraid."

They took time to savor their dinner, to laugh about possible career choices, and to enjoy chatting about restaurants, religion, politics, and their favorite Eric Clapton albums.

— Chapter 14 —

IT WAS PAST MIDNIGHT when Darryl returned to the small flat she shared with her friend from high school days, Kaycie Berringer. Thinking Kaycie asleep, she tiptoed past her bedroom when a voice called out, "It's about time you came home!"

Darryl stopped and opened her housemate's door. "What are you — my warden?"

"No." Kaycie sat up in bed, patted her short, brown hair into place, and frowned. Her nightshirt failed to hide the fifteen pounds she'd gained since their school days. "But I worry about you."

"Not to worry, sugarplum." Darryl leaned down and gave her a hug. "I'm a big girl, remember?"

Kaycie pulled away, still frowning. "Where were you? Were you with that guy you met in the sandwich shop?"

"Yup. After the party at his mother's fabulous

mansion, we went to dinner. Then we sat in his car and talked for two hours."

"About what?"

Disappointed that Kaycie didn't ask about the house, she replied, "Everything. Why the third degree?"

"Are you interested in the guy?"

"Damn right! Rob's the first bright, charming man I've met since my divorce. And he didn't pounce on me."

"I'll bet he kissed you goodnight."

Darryl sat down on the edge of the bed. "All right, Kace, spit it out. What's pissing you?"

"Nothing. Go to sleep."

"I'm not leaving till you tell me." Darryl crossed her arms and pretended to wiggle into a comfortable position.

"Okay, okay. I love you."

"I love you, too."

A tear rolled down Kaycie's cheek. "You say you love me. Why would you be attracted to him when you're living with me?"

Darryl's eyes widened in surprise. "You can't be serious. There's a friendship 'I love you' and a hormone 'I love you.' They're quite different."

More tears.

Darryl scratched her head and stood up. "You're delusional, Kace. I'm going to bed. You'll forget this crap in the morning."

— Chapter 15 —

KAYCIE DID NOT FORGET. Darryl was reading the newspaper

at breakfast, when her flat-mate came to the table. Her eyes were red and swollen.

"Dear God!" exclaimed Darryl. "Sit down, Kace. I'll make you some coffee."

"No — no, thanks. I guess we have to talk."

Darryl folded the newspaper and set it aside. "What's going on?"

"I'm sorry. I didn't mean to upset you." Not getting a comment, she continued, "I was a good athlete in school, remember? I loved sports and never paid much attention to boys, or vice versa. They liked the pretty girls like you."

"Pat Barber had a crush on you."

She shrugged. "I had a crush on you, and we became friends. We lost touch when you got married, but I still loved you. When I heard about your divorce, I asked you to move in with me."

"I know all that. Where's this going? Are you trying to tell me you're gay?"

"I don't know. I've never had sex with a man or a woman, and I don't particularly want to. But I have strong feelings for you. I somehow want us to be together — forever."

"Whew!" Darryl let out a whistle, hoping her shock didn't show. "That's a sweet thought, Kace, but it's not going to happen. Maybe you should talk to a therapist and work this out."

"Do you hate me?"

"Oh, don't be silly. You knew I was only staying here till I could afford my own place."

"If I go to a therapist, will you stay?"

"I'll stay a short time, Kace, but you should start advertising for someone to share the rent."

"No!" With an angry cry, she broke into loud gasps, and ran, sobbing, out of the room.

— Chapter 16 —

ROB MARSH LOST no time calling Darryl the next morning, and inviting her for a walk along Crissy Field, a popular track of land fronting the Bay. The day was crisp and clear — the water, sparkling blue against a backdrop of the Golden Gate Bridge. They'd stopped to browse at The Warming Hut, a gift shop/cafe at the end of the trail.

"Did you know this area used to be an airfield?" Rob asked, peering down at a display of local history books. "It honors a pilot, Major Dana Crissy, who was killed in a plane race to the East Coast. His friend, Colonel 'Hap' Arnold was devastated by the crash and asked that the new Presidio airfield be named for him."

"Too bad he's not around to see it."

"Speaking of not being around, you seem sort of detached today. Did I do something to offend you?"

"It's not you." She perked up instantly. "I wasn't going to tell you this, but last night, when I got home, Kaycie, the gal I live with, told me that she's in love with me."

"Wow! Did you know she was gay?"

"I'm not sure she is. We've known each other since high school and I know she's had emotional problems, but she's on medication and I thought she was okay. This came out of the blue."

His eyebrows raised excitedly. "That's not all bad. There might be a vacancy in my apartment building. It's a great location on California Street, right near Grace Cathedral."

"Thanks, Rob. I couldn't afford a place on Nob Hill. But I am determined to move."

"I understand." He walked over to a pile of maroon-colored Crissy Field T-shirts, and held one in the air. "I'm buying this to cheer you up."

"You cheer me, Rob," she said, smiling. "I'm so glad I stopped for a sandwich."

PART 4

— Chapter 17 —

THE DAYS FOLLOWING Kaycie's confession were difficult for both women. Darryl had a full schedule, and Kaycie spent her days working in the florist shop her family owned, and tending plants in their small garden. When she and Darryl passed in the hallway, they barely spoke.

At the same time, Rob was busy Christmas shopping, practicing, learning new tunes on his guitar, and playing gigs around town. Yet no matter what he did, he couldn't stop thinking about Darryl. The attraction was far stronger than anything he'd felt for the woman he'd been living with in Santa Monica, and indeed, for any woman he'd ever known.

Aware of Rob's growing desires, as well as her own, Darryl knew she'd soon have to make a decision. In many ways, Rob was young for his age, yet he showed himself to be surprisingly mature about women. Perhaps because he'd been so frustrated by his mother's domination, he made sure that Darryl knew she was free to be herself with him. And after twelve years of being prisoner in a bad marriage, she welcomed that quality.

It was too soon to think ahead, yet she found it impossible not to wonder if they had a future. Time was moving fast and she wanted children — a family. If Rob ever became serious in his intentions, his mother would probably find out that her parents weren't socially prominent, and conclude that she wasn't good enough for her beloved son.

If so, so be it. She knew that Rob came from wealth, but that wasn't what drew her to him. She felt, in fact, a strong physical attraction that was new to her. A virgin when she'd married Wellman Swift, she had never been unfaithful, and hadn't cared enough to sleep with anyone since the divorce. Sex with Wellman had been mechanical and dutiful, and not particularly pleasurable. But Rob had awakened a wonderful new desire. And that pleased and excited her.

— Chapter 18 —

"YOU LOOK SENSATIONAL!" Rob Marsh let out a low whistle as he helped Darryl into his car. Once he'd told her they'd be having dinner with his mother and sister before the Symphony, she'd thought hard about what to wear, and ended up borrowing a black Oscar de la Renta dress from a friend. Small rhinestone earrings and a diamond brooch Wellman had given her for a wedding present were her only jewelry.

"I return the compliment," she smiled.

"I have to please Mumsy once in a while," he said, straightening his Hermès tie. "She paid over two hundred bucks for this thing. Can you imagine?"

"It's beautiful."

"No, you're beautiful. And speaking of same, you mentioned you were getting your hair colored, a manicure, pedicure, all those girl things. How did that go?"

"Fine. That was Monday. Tuesday, I had a fashion show. Had to walk in four-inch stilettos and they were killing me. Wednesday to Friday — today — was a trunk show at Neiman's, ten to three p.m., on my poor feet. And in between, I paid bills, cleaned house, and did errands."

"Did you take up knitting in your spare time?"

"I took up sleeping," she laughed.

"What's happening with your roommate?"

"Nothing, she's been very quiet." Time to change subjects. "Tell me more about tonight?"

He kissed her cheek. "It's going to be wonderful."

— Chapter 19 —

By the time they pulled into the Performing Arts Garage, Darryl knew that their destination was the Louise M. Davies Symphony Hall, across the street from the Opera House. She had often driven by and admired its striking semi-circular façade.

Rob showed their tickets at the door, took his date's hand, and led her into the Wattis Room, a private dining room for major donors. Colorful paintings adorned the walls and fresh flowers enhanced the décor. Rob was immediately recognized and shown to the Marsh table.

Darryl had no trouble spotting her host. A handsome, elegant woman with perfectly-coiffed gray hair and a commanding presence, Edith Marsh offered her cheek to her son, then smiled pleasantly.

"You must be the lovely Darlene I've heard about. Glad you could join us, my dear."

Rob frowned. "It's Darryl, not Darlene."

"Thank you, Mrs. Marsh." Darryl almost felt like curtseying. "You're so kind to include me."

With a dismissive wave of the hand, Madame indicated that Darryl was to sit next to her, on the left, with Rob on Darryl's other side. "Hallie and Mr. Casserly will be along soon," she added.

"Mr. Casserly? Mom, get over it!" Rob shook his head angrily. "He's a great guy and he's going to be your son-in-law in two months."

"We'll see, dear," she said.

Darryl gave a noticeable shiver. Family tensions among the wealthy were a new phenomenon. To her relief at not having to make small talk, Hallie and Cas arrived minutes later. Hallie kissed cheeks and introduced Cas to Darryl, who tried hard not to stare. But what a hunk! Gray-black hair and horn-rimmed specs did nothing to lessen his remarkable presence. No wonder Hallie was smitten.

Edith Marsh seated Cas on her right. Then she turned to Darryl. "How did you and Robbie meet?"

"The name's Rob," he interjected, then quickly added, "we met through mutual friends."

"How nice." Her son's glare told her that was the end of the interrogation. She paid no attention. "And I understand you're a model?"

Darryl pretended not to notice Rob's annoyance. "That's right, Mrs. Marsh. I've been lucky enough to find plenty of work and it pays the rent."

"Good for you, my dear. I've always valued independence."

"Yeah, sure," muttered Rob.

Hallie quickly interceded. "Mom, are you having any luck finding a new curator?"

"No, I'm thinking of placing an ad, maybe on Crane's list."

"Craigslist," said Hallie. "What would you say in the ad? How would you word it?""

His mother's attention thus diverted, Rob grabbed Darryl's hand under the table and squeezed it hard. She smiled to herself and squeezed back.

— Chapter 20 —

LOBSTER BISQUE and roast chicken were served promptly and efficiently. Darryl knew her table manners would be under scrutiny, and was grateful that modeling school had included a course in etiquette.

After dinner, the party of six proceeded up the stairs to Edith's box. The seats looked out at the stunning auditorium, with its floating plastic sound panels suspended from the ceiling. Behind the orchestra, metallic organ pipes glistened in the soft lights. Every chair was filled, even in the balconies.

Rob had told Darryl the program would feature the Preservation Hall Jazz Band, and "old-time New Orleans music." The visiting performers were welcomed with a standing ovation; the audience left happy and humming.

The highlight of the evening for Darryl had been when Hallie whispered in her ear, "I think you're great for my brother. Don't let Mumsy scare you."

"Wish I could invite you in for coffee, but the situation hasn't changed." Darryl gathered her coat and purse, as Rob pulled up to her flat in the Marina district, not far from Yacht Harbor. "Kaycie and I haven't spoken since yesterday."

He paused a moment, then asked hesitantly,

"Would you like to see my apartment? I promise not to attack you, though I've a hunch you can take care of yourself."

She laughed. "All I know is you don't go for the man's groin anymore, you go for his eyes. Thanks, I'd like to see where you live."

"Hey, fabulous!" Not waiting for her to change her mind, he switched directions and headed east, towards Nob Hill. Fifteen minutes later, he turned into a driveway off California Street. At the touch of a button, the garage door opened. He parked and helped her out of the car.

"We'll go in the back and bypass the doorman," he said. "The guy's too nosy."

— Chapter 21 —

DARRYL WAS HAVING SECOND THOUGHTS as they rode up in the elevator. She wanted Rob to kiss her, a real kiss, and she knew their mutual attraction was strong. So why had she agreed to see his apartment? Why had he taken pains to bypass the doorman? They would be alone and...the elevator stopped abruptly.

"Welcome to my humble digs," he said, opening the door and turning on the lights.

She gazed around in surprise. It was quite different from the apartments she'd been looking at. Thick wall-to-wall carpets led the way into a spacious living room. A lone oil painting hung over the marble fireplace. She recognized the flying figures, but couldn't think of the artist's name.

Two white leather couches and matching chairs

were grouped around a marble coffee table. Atop it sat an art book. She stared closer. Of course – Mark Chagall! The fireplace painting was on the cover. Could it possibly be the original?

Across the room, what appeared to be a wall of glass looked out on a small balcony. Just beyond, one could see the lights of the city, Alcatraz Island, and the Bay.

"Hallie helped me decorate," Rob said. "She's a minimalist. Hates clutter."

"So I see. She has terrific taste."

He helped her out of her coat, slipped off his jacket and unbuttoned his collar. "What may I offer you? Coffee? Tea? Me?"

"You," she wanted to reply. He looked so damn attractive with his open shirt and loosened tie. "Thanks, I'm not thirsty."

"Good, I'm not either." He took her hand and led her to the sliding glass door. "Too cold to go outside for a minute?"

"Let's try."

The night air was clear and cool, the moon almost full, and the panorama exhilarating. He put his arm around her and felt her snuggle closer. "Freezing?"

"Not yet. What a charming sculpture!" She peered down at a small metal figure. "Who was the artist?"

"Ever heard of Lattrini Obscutepazzi?" He spelled the name and repeated it.

"There was a boy in grammar school with a name like that."

"Was he tall and dark?"

"No, short and blond." She paused a few seconds, then looked up at him with a twinkle. "It must have been some other Lattrini Obscutepazzi."

He caught her eye and started to laugh. She giggled back and soon they were in hysterics. Every time they tried to stop, they'd look at each other and start again. It seemed almost uncontrollable. Finally, he pulled her to him and held her head against his chest till she could laugh no more. Then he tilted her chin, leaned down and gently brushed her lips.

She responded instantly, reaching her arms around his neck. It seemed so right. So natural. Her feelings took over and she had no desire to stop them. In seconds, they were kissing with an urgency neither had known before.

He broke away for an instant, walked her inside, and closed the glass door behind them. Then he lifted her in his arms and carried her down the hall. "My beautiful Darryl," he whispered. "Tonight is ours."

— Chapter 22 —

DESPITE ROB'S PLEAS to stay for breakfast, Darryl insisted she had to be home before dawn. It was still dark at four a.m. when he drove her to her flat. She sat close to him in the car, her hand resting on his thigh. It's infatuation, she told herself, great sex doesn't mean love.

"When will I see you?" he asked, as they approached their destination.

"I'll call you when I check my calendar." Her voice softened. "In case I haven't told you, last night was wonderful in every way."

"For me, too. But I'm afraid my passion took over and I wasn't careful. You may want to take the morning-after pill."

"I think I'm okay. When I was first married, I tried to get pregnant. I did all the right things and nothing happened. So I'm not too worried."

"Of course that's up to you. All I know is that I've never wanted any other woman the way I wanted you — and still do. I lived with a gal in Santa Monica. She was a good woman, but I never loved her. It's different with you."

She let that remark slip by. "Here we are at my place, Rob. Thanks for everything. I'll just let myself out."

"No, wait, I'll come around and get you. Promise to call? Soon?"

"I promise." Before he could open his door, she jumped out of the car and ran up the stairs.

— Chapter 23 —

KAYCIE WAS AWAKE when Darryl arrived home, and called out to her. She entered her friend's bedroom. "Hope I didn't wake you."

"No. Got a minute?"

"Sure." Exhausted as she was, Darryl sat down on the bed.

"I'm sorry I offended you."

"Kaycie, dear, it's okay. Let's give it a rest and be friends again."

"Really? You forgive me?"

Darryl leaned forward and hugged her. "Nothing to forgive. Now let's both get some sleep. I'm pooped."

Kaycie pulled slightly away. "I know what you've been doing. And I forgive you."

Forgive me? For what? She wondered.

"Do you think you'll get pregnant?"

"Good Lord, no!"

"It'd be wonderful for us to have a baby together."

Oh shit, she thought. "I'm not having any baby, Kace. And what the hell is that black thing?"

Kaycie grinned. "I wanted to surprise you for Christmas." She reached under her pillow. "It's a Glock 38 pistol — what the cops use. Isn't she a beauty?"

"No!" Darryl jumped up in horror. "Where'd you get that? You know I hate guns!"

"I bought it at a gun show. It's perfectly safe. I take all precautions. I went to a pistols class and I've been shooting at the range every day. I want to be able to protect you — and our baby."

"Goddamnit, there's no baby! And I won't have a gun in the house!" Pale with shock and anger, Darryl slammed the door and fled to her room.

— Chapter 24 —

ROB TWISTED AND TURNED IN HIS SHEETS, unable to sleep. A night of intense lovemaking kept his adrenalin flowing. It seemed as if they'd both unleashed each other's secret passions. Darryl had told him she'd never been with anyone but her husband, and he believed her. At first she'd been timid, even modest. The room had to be dark, their mating literally "under cover." It took all his restraint to satisfy her, but he did. He wondered if she'd ever had an orgasm with Wellman.

She initiated their second time. She seemed hungry for him and suddenly came alive. The new Darryl was a hot, sexy woman who moaned with pleasure and couldn't get enough of him. The feeling was mutual — and unbelievably wonderful.

He had, however, a day's work ahead of him. They had an important gig that evening; he was even getting paid a hundred bucks, which didn't always happen.

True to her word, Darryl had phoned and they'd made a date for the afternoon of Christmas Eve. He'd wanted to meet sooner, but she was cautious, and didn't want to seem too eager. She assured him that when she wasn't working, she was out hunting for an apartment.

Darryl and Rob spent most of their tryst talking. She wanted to know more about him, and had mentally prepared a slew of questions. He sensed that she didn't share his desire to hop right into bed, answered her briefly, and restrained his libido as long as he could.

Yes, he told her, he practiced two to four hours every day. If he played longer than four hours, he'd have muscle problems.

Other parts of his day he spent listening to music, updating his website with new gigs, press announcements, and videos featuring him and his various bands. He would also be looking for work, contacting other musicians to set

53

up rehearsals, and reading the latest music news, along with more general matters, such as tracking his investments and tending to life's necessities. He tried to visit his mother once a week, but didn't always make it.

When he could no longer hold back, he simply said, "Enough talking," and took her in his arms. There was no resistance.

— Chapter 25 —

THAT EVENING, Christmas Eve, Rob joined his family for dinner, Kaycie went off to spend the weekend with her family, and Darryl drove to Piedmont to dine at her childhood home with her father, Stewart Woods, and stepmother Brenda.

Darryl was pleased that Brenda had kept most of her mother's furnishings. Except for the oversized TV and the bookshelves stacked with CD's and DVD's, the living room still seemed old-fashioned and cozy.

As usual, Brenda wore too much makeup, her hair was too red, and her tight green dress offered an abundance of cleavage. How she'd changed from the quiet, mousy file clerk her father had fallen for and married! In her fifties now, she'd learned to make the most of her features: large brown eyes, a strong but inoffensive nose, and a less-than-perfect complexion she covered with foundation. The overall effect was passable, especially when she smiled.

Her husband, Stewart, was bright and twinkly-eyed, with thinning white hair and matching moustache. He'd always been a ladies' man, and the ladies, in turn, responded to his good-natured flirting. When criticized, he liked to say, "I'm married, I'm not dead!" Perhaps Brenda was simply trying to keep up with the competition.

Darryl kissed her stepmother perfunctorily. Then, spotting champagne on the coffee table, she filled a glass and dropped into a chair. Brenda took a seat on the couch opposite her, and Stewart gingerly joined her.

"Your father had a bad spill last week," Brenda said, explaining his slow motion.

"What happened, Dad?" Darryl turned to her father in concern. He was over sixty, and had health problems he refused to talk about.

"Nothing, dear," he said quickly. "Your stepmother likes to exaggerate."

A glare from her husband snapped Brenda to attention. "Oh, I didn't mean it was serious. We've just had to stay home a lot and I get a bit stir-crazy."

"I understand," said Darryl, who didn't understand at all. What wouldn't she give for some quiet leisure time at home. "I just wish you'd tell me what's going on."

Stewart smiled. "I'm alive, well, and we must all count our blessings."

Brenda smiled back. "I agree. You can have champagne, Stew, it's only three or four carbs a glass."

"Carbs? Dad, are you dieting?"

"No," he said firmly, "and that's enough of the third degree. Tell us about your glamorous life. Now that you're unattached, are you meeting any young men?"

"I guess I'm meeting them," she laughed. "I'm not liking them much. Well, I did meet someone nice." Damn, she thought. She hadn't intended to say anything.

"Oh?" Brenda's eyes widened. "Who is he? What does he do?"

Too late to escape. "Mostly, he plays the guitar. Doesn't make much of a living at it, but he's sweet and sensitive."

"How did you meet?"

"Mutual friends," she replied, echoing Rob's answer to the same question. It was no one's business that they "picked each other up" in a sandwich shop.

"Have you met his family?" Brenda persisted. She seemed to sense Darryl was holding back.

"Yes, he has a darling sister, Hallie. His late father was an art collector, and his mother's a bit snooty. She has some nice paintings." It tickled her to call that fantastic collection "nice."

"What's your young man's name?" asked Stewart.

"Rob Marsh, Daddy, and he's not 'my' young man. We haven't known each other long, so it's nothing serious."

"Too bad," teased Brenda. "I have no children, as you know, so you're our only hope for grandchildren. Why didn't you bring him tonight?"

"He's having dinner with his family and I'm having dinner with mine." Her tone left no doubt that the subject was over. She glanced at the antique clock on the mantel, and marveled that it still worked. Three hours to go before Rob could get away from his dinner and meet her at his apartment. It would be a long three hours.

— Chapter 26 —

DARRYL WAS IN NO HURRY to leave Rob's bed the next morning. The sky was dark and overcast, the snuggling addictive. "Are you awake?" he whispered.

"Mmm — sort of," she mumbled.

"Good." He leaned across her to grab a small box on the bed table. Then he set it on her pillow. "Merry Christmas, darling."

Darryl looked up in surprise. "I thought we agreed no gifts."

"I lied."

"Not fair." Still half-asleep, she slipped the wrapping paper off a suede-covered box. It looked expensive, and for a moment she wondered if it held a ring. She hoped not. It was much too soon.

Her apprehension vanished a moment later. Inside the box was a handsome watch surrounded by stones that looked suspiciously like diamonds.

"Rob —" she gasped, "It — it's gorgeous! But —"

"Shush," he said, finding her lips. "It's for a gorgeous woman I'm crazy about. Wear it in good health, sweetheart. Would you feel better if I told you Hallie helped pick it out? She said you can take it back to Neiman's if you don't like it."

"I love it!" Darryl lifted her arm and fastened the strap.

"The salesperson told us Dianne Feinstein wears a watch like this. That was all Hallie needed to hear. She's a big fan of the Senator's. Anyway, I set it to the right time and you never have to wind it."

"Really?" Darryl gazed at her wrist, almost speech-less. Then she spoke softly. "Thank you, dear Rob, I'll treasure this almost as much as I treasure you."

Shortly after ten, Darryl and Rob sat at breakfast, downing coffee and sweet rolls and reading the Sunday *New York Times* "just like old married folk," he noted. Then the phone rang.

"I'm not home," he said.

"It might be your mother."

"Oh — okay." He lifted the receiver and heard a strange female voice. Then he handed the phone to Darryl. "It's for you."

"Me? No one knows I'm here except —" She answered nervously. "Kaycie?"

"Hi sweetie, hope I'm not disturbing anything. I just want to wish you Merry Christmas."

"Uh — same to you. Where are you?"

"I'm with my family. Was that Rob? He sounds nice."

"Yes. Is something wrong?"

"No, I just want you to know I'm thinking about you."

"Thanks, Kace. I'll see you tomorrow." She hung up hastily and shook her head, wondering if she should mention the gun, then decided against it. The weapon would soon be gone. "My friend gets weirder all the time."

"I don't like it, Darryl. I get funny vibes from her. It's time you got the hell out of there."

PART 5

— Chapter 27 —

New Year's Eve

THE WEEK AFTER Christmas, Darryl spent most of her days at St. Anthony's Dining Room, serving meals to the hungry and homeless, along with helping in the administrative office. She and Rob tried to squeeze each other into their busy schedules, and for the moment, she wasn't thinking about moving. Kaycie was behaving, had put the gun in her safe deposit box, and promised to get rid of it as soon as possible. They had no immediate problems and little communication.

Rob had insisted on cooking dinner that Friday evening, the last night of the year. Darryl dressed with an aching heart. She would do her best to seem and sound normal, but her fears had come true that morning, and she had no choice but to tell him.

The apartment looked spectacular, she told Rob, after parking in his garage and arriving around six. Tiny red apples and peppermint sticks decorated a tall Christmas tree. Behind it spread the panorama of the city, hundreds of lights flickering against a black, starless sky.

Candles lit a small table by the glass doors to the balcony. Rachmaninoff played on the stereo. As they sat sipping wine and eating the steaks he'd cooked, he spoke about his career hopes for the future. Then he paused to set down his fork. "And the lovely Darryl? Does she have plans for the New Year?"

"Yes, she does," she replied, trying to sound cheerful.

He picked up her tone instantly. "What is it, honey? I can tell when something's bothering you."

"It — can wait. I don't want to spoil the evening."

"I'm not as fragile as I look." He reached across the table for her hand. "Please?"

She nodded assent, having already decided to be honest. Then she said quietly. "I missed my period."

His face froze as he withdrew his hand. "When?"

"Two days ago. I've always been right on schedule. So I bought a digital pregnancy test. It's supposed to be a hundred percent reliable if you use it on the first or second day of a missed period. It — was positive."

"Couldn't the test be wrong? We've been so careful...except for that first night."

"I'm afraid not. My body feels different already. My breasts are getting tender."

He exhaled deeply. "I — I don't know what to say."

"You don't have to say anything. No one needs to know. It's my fault and I'm having it taken care of."

He looked up, startled. "You — you're getting an abortion?"

"Yes. You told me you were pro-choice and that's my choice."

The room was silent for a moment. Darryl's heart was racing as she set down her napkin and stood up. "I'm sorry. I should have told you before you went to all this trouble. I'd better go."

"No, wait. Let me think." He closed his eyes and pressed his lips together — a gesture she'd come to recognize when he faced decisions. She wanted to protest, to tell him it wasn't his problem, but he was deep in concentration. After a few minutes, he came around the table and took her hands. "I'm pro-choice when the pregnancy isn't wanted, but — golly, Darryl, I don't want to lose our baby. You said you wanted to have children, remember?"

"I'm thinking about you — your mother — Hallie — how will they feel about it?"

"I don't care, darling. Mumsy will have a stroke or two, that's for sure. But Hallie will be thrilled. She told me today that she's never seen me happier."

"I — don't know —"

"Okay, then, I'll marry you. We'll keep it legal and legitimate."

Her face reflected surprise, then sudden annoyance. "That's noble of you, Rob, but I would never marry you under these conditions."

"Okay," he said, almost angrily. "Don't marry me. But please, Darryl, if you care about me at all, don't lose our baby!"

"I'm sorry. I've got to rethink everything." She grabbed her coat from the closet and hurried out the door.

— Chapter 28 —

HER EYES RED FROM CRYING, Darryl paid the cab driver, and entered her flat to find Kaycie standing in the kitchen, stirring a pot. "Smells good," she said, sniffing.

Kaycie glanced at the clock. "Why are you home so early? Are you okay?"

"I'm okay."

"I think you need a hug." Kaycie's arms wrapped around her before she could object. "Everything's going to be fine, just fine," she whispered. "I'm here, you're here, and I'll take care of you — forever."

"Thanks. You're a good friend." Pulling away, Darryl began sobbing. "I'm such a darn fool, Kace. I've hurt the only man I've ever really cared about. I've made such a mess of things."

"Don't cry. Please don't cry." Kaycie's voice was soft and soothing. "Was Rob mad because you're pregnant?"

"How did you know?"

"I saw the test papers in your waste basket. Then it all made sense — why you've been so cold to me. I know you care about me, so there had to be a reason."

"Of course I care about you, just not romantically."

"I understand. And I promise I won't bug you any more. I can help you through your pregnancy. I really want that baby."

Darryl shivered. "I can't make any decisions now. I'm taking a sleeping pill and going to bed."

— Chapter 29 —

THE PHONE RANG EARLY the next morning. Caller ID told Darryl it was Rob. She let it ring. He called three more times that hour and she continued to ignore him. How could she think rationally if he were pressuring her?

The fifth call Darryl saw who it was and answered. "Hi, Hallie. Happy New Year."

"What the hell's going on, Darryl? You sound awful and Rob's ready to jump off the bridge. He won't tell me anything."

"He's protecting me." She sighed. "I made the mistake of telling him I'm pregnant. I should've just taken care of it and he'd never have known."

"I suspected as much. You did exactly the right thing. Look, are you dressed?"

"No."

"Well, put on your jeans and a warm coat. I have your address. I'll pick you up in half an hour and we'll go to Crissy Field."

The idea of visiting the spot where she'd been so happy with Rob made Darryl burst into tears. "I'll be ready," she sniffed, wiping her eyes.

The rain had stopped, temporarily, but dark clouds lingered over the Golden Gate Bridge. It felt unusually cold for San Francisco, thought Hallie, as they strolled by the water. The deep, penetrating chill cut right through her coat and three sweaters. Whoever said, "There's no bad weather; only bad clothes," was wrong.

She listened closely as Darryl recounted the events of the preceding evening. Then she announced, "You're right, my brother acted like a jerk. No woman wants a man who says, 'I'll marry you,' as if he's doing you a favor."

"He meant well. But how could I possibly marry a man I've known three weeks? And besides, your family's so prominent, people would think I'd purposely gotten pregnant."

Hallie shrugged. "You have two choices. Either abort the baby or keep it."

Darryl had to smile. "Thanks, Dr. Einstein."

"Seriously. Do you want the baby?"

"More than anything."

"Then what's the problem? This is twenty-eleven, remember? Women who want babies have babies. Then they can decide if they want the daddies to be in the picture."

"It's not that simple, not with your family."

"Listen." Hallie took her arm as they walked. "When I started my own business, my mother supported me, even though she was horrified. Her daughter working as a common press agent? I might as well have joined a brothel."

"Your mother's of a different generation."

"That's for sure. But I felt I had to prove myself. So I got a few clients, I'd sneak their name into a column or two, orchestrate a media mention if I could, think up dumb stunts and newsworthy events, and voila! I was successful."

"I know. I saw your website."

"And I saw your agency's website with your picture. Glad we checked each other out." They laughed. "One day I realized that some of my clients only hired me for their egos and their fifteen minutes of fame, or else to try to sell their phony products. One client had an anti-wrinkle cream that did absolutely nothing, another had a glue that claimed to hold up stockings, but didn't. I was spending hours promoting these con artists, and it wasn't making the world any better."

"I'd like to help the world, too. But I need to work to pay my rent. And very few jobs call for a pregnant model."

"Okay, bottom line: Today, about half our work is

pro bono, for people and charities in need. We get their benefits listed in every possible publication, we get their leaders interviewed, we promote their cause, and we don't charge them a cent. It's true, your modeling career will have to go on hold, but Ken, my right hand at the office, wants to spend six months in Europe, and I've been putting off finding a replacement. Do you know when you're due?"

"September ninth."

"Perfect! Keep your bookings for another two or three months. I read somewhere that at eight weeks, your belly's only the size of a lemon. When you start to show, I'll hire you and pay you an equivalent salary. Don't argue," she said, before Darryl could protest. "I want that baby, too!"

— Chapter 30 —

KAYCIE BERRINGER WAS IN HEAVEN. She and her beloved Darryl were going to be parents! She could hardly wait to transform the storage area into the baby's room. Darryl almost never went in there. What fun it would be to surprise her!

But no hurry. She learned from Google that a pregnant woman should wait twenty weeks before having an ultrasound. Until then, the fetus's male and female sex organs look similar. After twenty weeks, however, the ultrasound will not only show the baby's sex, it will inform the parents of any health irregularities.

A girl. She was sure it would be a girl. She would start looking at stores on her day off. Or maybe she could order online. Pink curtains would be perfect for the room's only window. The crib would go right beside it.

She prayed Darryl wouldn't get sick in the morning the way some women do. Still, her parents' florist shop would survive if Darryl needed her to stay home. The way men looked at Darryl was scary. You could see they had bad thoughts.

Darryl needed to be protected. Kaycie was glad she'd gone to the safety deposit box and secretly retrieved her gun. It was safe, now. She'd hidden it in a fake book on the shelf with all her mystery novels. Darryl would never find it.

— Chapter 31 —

AFTER A TALK WITH HER BROTHER, Hallie felt confident the situation could be resolved. Rob had been crushed by Darryl's reaction to his offer; he had never proposed to anyone before. Even if her pregnancy had forced him to do it, he felt certain he was still a "good catch." Why didn't she want him? Why had she been so turned off?

He guessed she blamed him for the Dastardly Deed, but Hallie said no, Darryl blamed herself for not getting the "morning after" pill as he'd suggested. Women have pride, too, Hallie explained. Someone with Darryl's looks, charm, and smarts was not about to rush into marriage with a man she barely knew. She needed nurturing, she needed to know that she was loved for herself, that she'd be loved on bad hair days and screaming baby days, and that she wouldn't be a trophy wife again.

Rob had been somewhat appeased. He adored his sister, and sensed a surprising bond between the two women. Hallie didn't have that many close female friends, so her concern for Darryl pleased him.

— Chapter 32 —

FRUSTRATED that Darryl still wasn't answering the phone, Rob decided to drive to her house. It was almost dinner time; she would probably be home. Finding a parking spot a few blocks away, he walked briskly to her street, then up the steps to her front door. It occurred to him that he was looking fairly grubby in his sweatshirt and jeans. No matter. They had to talk.

Kaycie answered the doorbell. "Hi," he said. "I'm Rob Marsh. Sorry to disturb you but I need to speak to Darryl."

She ignored his outstretched hand. "You can't right now. She's sleeping."

"It's important. I really need to talk to her."

"I told you she's sleeping." Kaycie stood up to her full four-foot-ten inch height, and spread her arms, barring the way. "Now please quit bothering us and go home."

"Not until I see her." He pushed Kaycie aside and hurried down the hall. "Darryl," he yelled, "Where are you?"

A head poked out of a door. "Rob? Is that you? What's going on?"

"We need to talk. Please?"

She nodded, and tightened the sash to her bathrobe.

"Yes, yes, come in. I was just watching the news." He followed her into the small room they called the library, and joined her on the couch. "Hallie called and told me you were very sweet about everything," she said, switching off the TV. "Thank you."

"Darryl," he said gently, "I want us to have that baby. You can hate me all you want —"

"Good grief, I don't hate you! I just didn't want you to feel you had to marry me."

He grinned. "You mean it's settled? You'll have the baby?"

"Darn right she'll have our baby," interrupted Kaycie, standing in the doorway. Then, quite calmly, she reached up to the shelf where she'd hidden her gun in a fake book. Removing the weapon, she raised and aimed it. "Now get out of here, Mr. Rob Marsh, or I swear I'll pull this trigger."

Darryl jumped up. "Give me that gun, Kaycie! Are you out of your mind?"

"No! I won't let him rape you. That's what he came for. He just wants to rape you again. He has to leave — now!" A bullet sailed past Rob's shoulder, missing him by inches. Darryl screamed, rushed over and reached for the weapon. The women struggled. Within seconds, Rob came from behind and smacked Kaycie's back — hard. She fell forward, dropping the pistol to the floor. He snatched it and pointed it at Kaycie.

"Get dressed, Darryl," he ordered. "I'm not leaving you with this mad woman. You're coming with me."

— Chapter 33 —

AGAINST ROB'S WISHES, Darryl had helped Kaycie to her feet, given her a Prozac, which she was already taking every morning, and put her to bed. Calling from the other room, Rob spoke to his sister, Hallie, who insisted he bring Darryl there for the night.

Darryl at first objected, preferring to stay at a hotel, but he persuaded her that she shouldn't be alone. Hallie and Cas took them both for pizza and discussed what to do. After dinner, Rob would deliver the gun to the police, explaining that its owner was mentally unstable and should never have been sold the pistol. Darryl would call Kaycie's parents, which she did. The Berringers immediately went to get their daughter and bring her home with them.

The next night Darryl spent in Piedmont with her stepmom, Brenda, and her dad, telling them everything. They were worried, and urged her to get a restraining order, pointing out that Kaycie was seriously ill and could easily get another gun without a permit, possibly from a pawn shop or at a gun show. Darryl argued that a restraining order would be cruel and unnecessary.

In the meantime, Rob arranged for Darryl to move into a small unfurnished apartment in his building. The rent was so reasonable she suspected Rob was paying part of it, but he swore otherwise, explaining that the building's owner was a good friend.

Once she confirmed that Kaycie was spending a few days with her parents, Darryl packed up her belongings, called the furniture truck, and moved out.

PART 6

— Chapter 34 —

A WEEK PASSED. Hallie was in her office when Rob called, furious to learn that Kaycie had left her parents' house and moved back into her flat, when he felt she should be hospitalized. Darryl had talked him out of pressing charges for attempted murder, and Hallie had helped calm him, focusing on a more immediate problem: how to tell Mumsy she would be a grandmother. Rob hadn't wanted to subject Darryl to whatever his mother's reaction might be, but Hallie said Mumsy would be more civil if Darryl were present. (Cas wanted no part of the scene.)

Edith Marsh was delighted to learn that her children, and Rob's friend Darryl, wanted to dine with her that evening. Dinner was promptly at seven, and the three guests arrived early, meeting for drinks in the sitting room. Grimaldi, the butler, served Rob's favorite hors d'oeuvres, mini-hot dogs in pastry dough, and talk was light and pleasant.

The formal dining room with its long English Edwardian table and tall stiff chairs, did not lend itself to relaxing. Nevertheless, Hallie and Rob seemed happily at ease, while Darryl sat petrified.

As Grimaldi served the crab cocktails, the host turned to her daughter. "Is there some reason I'm being honored with my children's company tonight? You two — well, you three, I'm sure — are all very busy with your lives."

Before anyone could answer, she noticed Grimaldi removing a pair of wine glasses. "Darryl, would you prefer a soft drink or some juice?"

"No, thanks, Mrs. Marsh. I've never been much of a drinker. Water's fine."

"An excellent choice, my dear, although you seemed to enjoy your wine at our Symphony dinner. Are you feeling all right?"

Darryl swallowed nervously. "Er, well —"

"You've already guessed, haven't you, Mom?" said Hallie, with her usual directness. "You're going to be a grandmother."

"Good heavens!" Edith's eyes widened. She stared at her daughter, then her son. Were they teasing? A quick glance at Darryl's deep blush told the story.

The room was eerily silent for a moment, then the host lifted her glass. "In that case," she said, forcing a smile, "we have something to celebrate. When are you due, my dear?"

"Sep — tember, Mrs. Marsh. I assure you this was an accident."

"I have no doubt it was. You're a beautiful and charming young woman. You must have many suitors. Are you sure my son is the father?"

"Damn you, Mother!" Rob jumped to his feet. "C'mon, Darryl, we're getting out of here!"

"Oh, sit down, Rob," said Hallie. "Mom doesn't know the facts. It's a natural question. Now *sit* down!"

"Screw you, Hallie. She has no business insulting Darryl — or me." He stood scowling. His arms were folded, but his voice was calmer.

"Please sit down, Robbie," said Edith quietly. "My remark was uncalled-for. Will you forgive me, Darryl?"

Speechless, she simply nodded.

"Good. Then let's get down to business. We have to

start planning your wedding."

— Chapter 35 —

THANKS TO HALLIE'S organizing abilities and diplomacy skills, the family made some serious decisions at the dinner table. Darryl at first refused to get married, Rob remained neutral but willing, and both eventually gave in to Hallie's reasoning, and agreed — for the sake of the baby — to a private quickie wedding. Hallie promised Darryl that the family would support an equally quickie divorce after the baby was born — if that was her wish.

As they talked, Edith admitted that she was in constant pain, and had put off hip replacement surgery till after Hallie's wedding. Not one to miss an opportunity, Hallie jumped in and offered to forget the big hotel reception and have the ceremony be a private event at Mumsy's house.

She and Cas, Rob and Darryl would take their vows at the same time, without frills, without guests, and as soon as possible so the baby's birth would not raise questions — as if anyone cared anymore. Mumsy could schedule her surgery right after the weddings, and Cas would be thrilled. How he'd been dreading a big society reception!

They picked Friday for the ceremony, the first day Darryl had no bookings. Edith would arrange for boutonnieres, bridal bouquets, champagne and dinner. Darryl would invite her parents and hunt for a suitable dress. Rob would buy a new suit, and at some point, he and Darryl would pop over to Room 168 at City Hall, get a marriage license, then pick up a pair of wedding rings. Blood tests, he'd learned from a newlywed friend, were no longer required.

Hallie suggested Rob and Darryl get pre-nup agreements. They both refused, insisting money wasn't and wouldn't be an issue.

All that remained for Hallie was a call to their minister. But since the three of them weren't particularly religious, and Cas bordered on atheism, she had a better idea.

— Chapter 36 —

JUDGE PAUL DODSON was delighted to hear from "my savior," as he teasingly called the young woman who had come to his aid after the car accident. Unfortunately, he had court dates on Friday, so they moved the nuptials to Saturday.

During the week, Hallie and her thrilled fiancé firmed up their own plans. There was no time to arrange for a honeymoon, but they would start looking for a place to live, since Mumsy agreed to make good on her promise to buy them a house.

Rob and Darryl would stay where they were. Their relationship was friendly but still touchy. He phoned every night, and they joked about their "shotgun wedding." Although he was dying to see her, he knew better than to push. Time would bring them closer. He had every intention of making the marriage work.

The night before the wedding, Rob's phone rang shortly after eight. A voice said, "Hi, Rob. I'm Egan Frond, a friend of your sister's. She gave me your number. Got a minute?"

75

"Sure." Rob grabbed the remote and muted the TV.

"I know you're busy so I'll get right to the point. I play the flute and I'm told you're a fine jazz guitarist. My trio is playing at a champagne brunch this Sunday and my guitarist just called to say he's throwing up all over the place. It does not bode well, if you get my meaning."

"I do," Rob laughed.

"The gig's in a high end restaurant in the Financial District, SoleMio, They're just reopening after a long re-modeling, so most people don't know they're open. This is sort of a trial run for the brunch, so we may not have much of an audience."

"Who else is in your trio?"

"Just me and a stand-up bass player. And we need a sub desperately. Any interest?"

"You getting paid?"

"A hundred bucks each for three hours and free food. Not bad, huh?"

"Sounds reasonable." Rob paused to think. Sunday was the day after his wedding. Would he have a traditional wedding night? And if so, would he want to leave his bride? Probably not. On the other hand, she might not even spend the night with him. What the hell. Performing in a first class restaurant was a step up in his career.

"Sure, I'll do it," he said. "We playing the usual standards?"

"You bet, nothing tricky. Let's meet at 10:30, so we can set up and go over the song list. And hey, thanks. You're everything Hallie said you are."

"Thanks for thinking of me. I assume the restaurant

76

pays for our parking?"

"Hey, don't push your luck." Egan laughed. "But yeah, they do. See ya Sunday!"

— Chapter 37 —

THE BRIDES-TO-BE had gone shopping together. Darryl's admiration and affection for Hallie seemed to grow the more she saw of her. Hallie had become her idol, everything she wanted to be: decisive, direct, loyal, loving, and honest, even when it hurt. The Mark Twain motto she liked to quote: "When in doubt, tell the truth," was a good one.

A blue silk dress in Neiman Marcus's window had caught Hallie's attention some weeks earlier, and she'd bought it for her wedding. But Darryl had nothing in her closet that she cared to wear.

Hallie had shaken her head sideways at the first batch of dresses Darryl tried on in Neiman's, commenting that she looked fabulous in everything, so it was a tough decision. Not finding what they wanted, they'd visited every bridal shop on Union Square, from Azadeh to Jin Wang, finally popping into "Vintage Lives!" on Post Street.

Darryl's fashion-trained eyes landed on a soft pink Chanel suit still carrying its original $4300 tag. The current price was half, $2150. Darryl said it was more than she could pay, Hallie offered the owner $2,000. They compromised on $2075. Despite Darryl's protest, Hallie charged it to Mumsy, explaining that she'd been instructed to do so.

— Chapter 38 —

CAS HAD NO FAMILY, so the only guests at the wedding ceremony were Darryl's dad and stepmom, Stewart and Brenda Woods. Hallie, Cas, Edith, Brenda and Rob stared in stunned silence as Darryl entered the Marsh's living room on the arm of her beaming father. Her stately carriage, flowing black hair, and exquisite features made a spectacular vision.

"A goddess," murmured Hallie.

"*Another* goddess," corrected Cas.

Edith nodded approval, Brenda smiled happily, and Rob, too dazzled to speak, crossed the room quickly, took his bride-to-be's hand, and led her back to where Judge Dodson stood waiting.

The ceremony was a bit longer than expected. The Judge had started out praising Hallie for saving his life, for her work with nonprofits, and for the Marsh family's long history of philanthropy and contributions to the arts. He went on to extol Rob's musical talents, Darryl's grace and beauty, and Cas's journalistic awards and accomplishments.

The rest of the ceremony was routine, and when it was over, the new husbands kissed their new wives. Everyone hugged, and the Judge politely regretted he couldn't stay for dinner.

Stewart Woods was exuberant during the meal, and toasted his "handsome son-in-law." He drank too much champagne, but held it well. Hallie and Cas told about a house they'd seen; they were thinking of making an offer. Edith raised her glass to "my wonderful children" and to everyone's relief, made no mention of a grandchild.

Darryl was pleased that her stepmother had taken her suggestion to "tone down" her appearance, and looked quite presentable in a beige Liz Claiborne suit. Brenda knew enough to be quiet during dinner, and possibly following her husband's orders, only spoke when spoken to. Darryl was pensive, but seemed happy, while secretly wondering whether or not to spend the night with her husband.

A joyful Rob invited everyone to hear him play at the champagne brunch the next day. The Woods regretted. Brenda explained that Stewart had health problems, and although they were staying at the Fairmont, they were leaving for home early the next morning. Edith, Hallie, Cas and Darryl accepted with pleasure.

— Chapter 39 —

ROB AWOKE SHORTLY BEFORE NINE, thrilled that his new wife lay sleeping beside him. How serene she looked, he thought proudly, and how he loved her! He would do anything — whatever he could do — to make her happy.

Quietly, he climbed out of bed, downed a bowl of cereal, dressed for his gig, and wrote Darryl a note reminding her of the details of the brunch. He signed with a drawing of a heart. Not having met the other musicians, and not knowing the layout, he wanted to get to the restaurant early.

Darryl awoke to the sound of the door closing, and moments later, the phone rang. Hallie was on the line to say that she and Cas were picking up Edith, and could stop for her on the way. Darryl declined gratefully, saying she had something to do first, and would meet them at the restaurant. As soon as she clicked off, she called a number.

On the sixth ring, a sleepy voice answered. " 'Lo?"

"Kaycie, I'm so sorry! Did I wake you?"

"Oh, hi, Darryl." A deep yawn. "It's good to hear from you."

"I was calling to ask if I could come see you."

"Thanks, but — I'm fine." She sighed, slowly waking up. "I'm really good now. And thanks for contacting my parents. They got me to my doctor and he doubled my Prozac. I'm sorry for what I did."

"That's good to hear. Are you seeing any sort of therapist?"

"No, the medicine's really working. Why did you want to visit me?"

"I wanted to tell you some news." Darryl paused to consider her words, then thought about what Hallie would say. "I got married yesterday."

"So how come you didn't invite me to the wedding?"

Relieved that there was no explosion, Darryl answered, "We didn't invite anyone, Kace, just my parents. I wanted to tell you in person."

"That was nice of you, but you don't have to worry about me. I'm glad for you, and I hope you and Rob will be happy. Will I ever see you again?"

"Yes, for sure." Kaycie's calm reaction triggered a wave of guilt. Impulsively, Darryl said, "Since you couldn't be there yesterday, why not come with me to brunch today? You can meet Hallie and her husband; they got married, too. And you can hear Rob play."

"Oh, no thanks, I —"

"C'mon, Kace. Put on your navy blue pantsuit, you look great in that. I'll pick you up at ten-forty-five. We'll sit together, I promise. Don't forget, I'll be needing you pretty soon as a babysitter."

Mentioning the baby had its effect. "Oh, well, in that case, okay, I guess. Are you sure?"

"Yes, I'm sure. Now go get dressed. I'll honk twice."

— Chapter 40 —

DRIVING TO HER FORMER FLAT to pick up Kaycie, Darryl tried to digest all that was happening in her life. The week had flown by — making preparations, the ceremony itself, the dinner, and then, afterwards. Rob had so sweetly asked her to stay with him on their "wedding night," assuring her that if she didn't want to, he would understand.

Buoyed by the happiness around her, Mumsy's and her parents' relief that their grandbaby would be legal, and Hallie and Cas's elation at finally being married, Darryl hugged Rob and whispered, "Yes" in his ear. The mood carried over to the bedroom. Their lovemaking was tender and joyful, and she fell asleep in his arms. Maybe this marriage could work after all.

Kaycie was waiting on the steps when Darryl drove up to the flat, and reached to open the car door for her.

"I'm moving like a turtle today," Kaycie mumbled, as she dragged herself onto the seat. "It's good to see you."

"You, too. Looks like you're taking a lot of Prozac."

"I'm taking twenty milligrams a day, a relatively low dose. Some people start at forty or sixty milligrams. I'm just feeling tired; I don't know why. Tell me where we're going?"

Darryl filled her in on details, and they soon pulled up to the striking stone façade of SoleMio, where a valet took the car.

Inside the restaurant, a maitre d' walked Darryl and Kaycie to the head of a stairway. To the right was a small balcony, where the three musicians were tuning their instruments. Not wanting to bother them, the pair headed down to a large room filled with banquettes and empty tables (except for one), covered with crisp white cloths. Soft light came from giant clam shell fixtures suspended from the ceiling. The effect was both startling and dramatic.

Darryl caught a wave from Hallie, seated with Cas and Edith, and headed towards them, holding onto Kaycie, who was having trouble walking.

Remembering the gun incident, Hallie and Cas hid their surprise and greeted the unexpected guest politely but coolly.

Unaware of Kaycie's history, Edith rejected Darryl's offer to sit by themselves; their round table could easily accommodate another person. The waiter was quick to bring an extra chair and place setting.

"Kaycie's my former housemate and good friend from high school, Mrs. Marsh," Darryl explained. "She was sad to miss the wedding so I thought she might enjoy coming here today. I hope you don't mind."

"Not at all, my dear. And now that you're in the

family, perhaps you should call me something other than Mrs. Marsh. How about Edith?"

"That's very thoughtful." Darryl smiled. "I'll try to get used to it."

At that moment, Rob looked down from the balcony and caught Darryl's eye. He pointed at Kaycie with a questioning look. What was his wife doing with the woman who'd tried to kill him?

She nodded up at him, forming a circle with her thumb and finger to indicate all was well. He frowned, and turned away.

Across the floor, a group of six appeared and took a table. "That's Leah and Jerry Frond, and their daughters and husbands," said Edith. "I wonder what brings them here?"

"Their son Egan invited Rob to play today," Hallie reminded her. "He's the flutist in the group."

"Yes, of course. We must stop and say hello before we leave."

PART 7

— Chapter 41 —

A CLOCK SOMEWHERE in the restaurant chimed eleven times, the trio opened with, "All the Things You Are," and the waiter announced that the buffet awaited the customers. In the rear of the room, a long table held four steel bins of hot foods, mainly egg dishes and pancakes. A second spread offered salads, vegetable dishes and desserts, and a top-hatted chef stood at yet another table, ready to slice hot turkey and roast beef.

Edith gave the go-ahead to her guests, and since Hallie and Darryl were busy talking, Cas, known for being perennially hungry, excused himself and headed for the buffet. The others soon followed. He came back to an empty table, except for Kaycie, who was slumped down in her seat. "Are you all right?" he asked.

She nodded. "I'm sorry, I can't seem to stay awake. My doctor doubled my medication and I'm feeling woozy. Could I please have some coffee?"

"Yes, sure." He signaled the waiter. "Would you like to lie down? Maybe there's a couch in the ladies' room."

"I — think the coffee will help."

By the time the women returned with their plates of food, Kaycie's head was bent to her chest, and she appeared to be snoozing soundly. Embarrassed, Darryl was about to wake her, when Edith intervened. "Let her sleep, poor dear. Hallie tells me she's been depressed about your moving out."

"Yes," Darryl answered, "she has been depressed. I don't know if her medication helps or makes it worse."

Attention turned to the excellent trio, now serenading the guests with "My Favorite Things." Chatter centered on movies, football coaches, and the upcoming Ballet Opening.

A couple with a teenage son wandered in, checked out the buffet and took a table. Business was not good, but as Darryl reminded everyone, few people knew the restaurant had reopened.

At noon, the trio took a fifteen-minute break. Rob, Egan, and Scotty, the bassist, came down to the restaurant to a round of family applause. Rob greeted his relatives, then asked if he and Darryl could talk privately.

Alone in a corner of the room, he pointed to the dormant Kaycie. "Why the hell did you bring her?"

"I'm sorry, Rob. She was upset that she wasn't invited to our wedding. I know it doesn't make sense to you after what she did, but she's emotionally sick and depressed, and she's really a good person. I wanted to show her that we forgive her."

"Shit, I don't forgive her! If that bullet had been two inches closer, our baby wouldn't have a father. She should be locked up and the key thrown away!"

"But she's on double medication now. She's so drugged she can't even stay awake. She couldn't harm an ant."

"Your judgment sucks," he growled, and strode off to rejoin his fellow musicians.

— Chapter 42 —

SHORTLY AFTER ONE, the Marsh family was getting ready

to leave, and Darryl was about to awaken Kaycie, when a woman's cries made everyone stop and stare across the room.

"Good Lord, that's Leah Frond!" exclaimed Edith. "Something's wrong with Jerry!"

Cas jumped up and hurried over to the table where a pale, older man sat clutching his chest, gasping for breath. Hallie ran behind him.

"Heart attack!" Cas cried out, "Call 911!"

The man's daughter grabbed her cell phone; his wife, Leah, began wiping his forehead.

"Anybody got aspirin?" asked Cas.

"Yes!" Leah dug into her purse, pulled out a silver box and extracted a pill. "Here, Jerry," she said, pushing it into his mouth, and offering him water. He seemed oblivious, still struggling to breathe.

"Get him to the floor," ordered Cas. Hallie and the two sons-in-law helped lay the victim on the rug. Slipping off his sweater, Cas folded it and placed it under the man's head. "Can you breathe, sir?"

"C-c-cardiac," he finally got out.

"Don't try to talk, Dr. Frond. And don't panic. Everything's under control. Hallie, raise his legs so blood flows to his heart. And please, everyone stand away and stay calm."

No sooner had he spoken, than the victim gave a sudden throaty gargle. His eyes rolled back and his head dropped to the side.

Leah screamed. "Oh, my God!"

Not losing a second, Cas started chest compressions.

He knew that the old mnemonic of ABC — Airway, Breathing, Compressions — had changed to CAB — Compressions, Airway, Breathing. Airway no longer came first. The rescuer could waste thirty critical seconds searching the mouth for obstructions.

After about ten minutes of intense compressions, Cas paused to lift the doctor's chin and run his fingers around the teeth and gums. Then he took a deep breath, pinched the man's nose closed, pressed down on his lips and blew.

Pausing only to breathe, he continued blowing, occasionally glancing to the chest. A slight rise and fall showed that air was getting through. When he stopped, however, he could see that Dr. Frond was not breathing on his own.

Back he went to the compressions, rotating them with occasional mouth-to mouth action. He continued for ten more minutes, until, to everyone's relief, three men — a Captain, a paramedic, and a firefighter — came dashing down the stairs, followed by Rob, Scotty, and a white-faced Egan Frond.

Cas rose quickly as the firefighter took over, and began compressing. The paramedic cut open the victim's shirt and stuck two patches on his chest.

Seconds later, the ambulance crew arrived, including two men carrying a gurney. They dropped it; one relieved the firefighter and continued the CPR, pausing every few minutes to read heart rhythms on the patches. A woman paramedic inserted a tube in the man's throat, and squeezed a device to blow air into his lungs. A third paramedic attached an IV, sending medication into the vein.

The team continued to work in unison, sharing results and commands, as vomit and body fluids spilled out of the man's mouth. The female paramedic looked questioningly at her co-worker.

"No rhythm, no pulse," he said. They silently agreed the automatic defibrillator wouldn't be needed.

After what seemed an eternity, the co-worker checked his watch, stopped the compressions, wiped his forehead, and stood up. He gave a nod to the others. "It's been twenty minutes," he said. "Call the M.E."

"What's happening?" cried Egan. "What's an M.E.?"

"The Medical Examiner." Cas grabbed him and held him back. "Calm down, Egan. Your father's at peace. Your mother and your sisters need you now."

— Chapter 43 —

BY THE TIME the Medical Examiner arrived, the Marsh family had joined the Fronds in tears and condolences. While they were embracing, Hallie took Cas aside. "Seems strange," she whispered. "According to his wife, Dr. Frond had no history of heart problems. She said he'd recently had a checkup, and except for arthritis and a bad knee, he assured her he was in good health."

Cas smiled. "Sweetheart, I know you always worry about foul play but he was a respected brain surgeon."

"He wrote a very controversial book last year, 'Fakes, Frauds, and Fables.' It was all about scams and psychics and con artists, and he named names. There were lawsuits. He had enemies."

"All the more reason to think stress caused his heart attack. Let's wait to hear from the M.E. Isn't he a friend of yours?"

"An acquaintance, Dr. Thomas Toy. He's a good man — a forensic pathologist."

"Then there's sure to be an autopsy." Cas glanced back to their table. "Is Kaycie still sleeping in her chair?"

"Darryl went to check. I'll go look."

Hallie quickened her steps across the room, arriving as a frantic Darryl was shaking Kaycie's shoulders. "She hasn't moved since we left her! I can't wake her!"

Hallie gave a hard slap on the back, and Kaycie slid off her chair to the floor, where she lay immobile. Dr. Toy, the Medical Examiner came running over. He dropped down, felt for a neck pulse, then rolled back her eyelids and shined a flashlight. "How long has she been sitting here?"

"Almost two hours," Hallie answered, fearing the worst. "We — thought she was sleeping."

"Sorry." He shook his head. "She's been dead at least an hour."

"Dead? That's not possible!" Tears streamed down Darryl's cheek. "She was fine today — just drowsy from her medication."

"Kaycie's dead, too?" Rob was right there to put his arms around his wife. "I'm so sorry, darling. I can't believe we have *two* bodies!" With a tearful nod, she buried her head in his shoulder and began to sob.

"Let's go home," he whispered, grabbed her coat and purse, and led her off. "I don't think they'll want any more music today."

PART 8

— Chapter 45 —

HALLIE ANSWERED all the officers' questions, requesting that both deaths be investigated. Cas asked that the report go to their friend, police Lieutenant Helen Kaiser. Mention of her name brought new respect. The police took copious notes and left.

A call that evening worried Hallie. Darryl phoned to report that she and Rob had stopped to see Kaycie's parents, the Berringers, and deliver the dreadful news. They took it badly, as expected, first blaming Darryl for moving out and causing Kaycie's depression. Rob was tempted to tell about the gun incident, but a look from Darryl stopped him.

"When I mentioned Kaycie was drowsy this morning," Darryl told Hallie, "the Berringers went ballistic. They said I shouldn't have 'made' her go to the brunch. Then they tried to blame the doctor and the medication. Finally, her father convinced her mother that it was God's will, and the Good Lord had His reasons for taking their daughter. Kaycie had told me they're quite religious."

"Let's hope that helps them get through this." Hallie sighed. "You did the right thing getting there before the police. Cas heard it on the radio this afternoon. They made a big deal of Dr. Frond's untimely death at sixty-two. They couldn't resist mentioning Kaycie's unexpected demise at thirty-two — 'daughter of longtime local florists, etc.' — and that both died unexpectedly at the same time and place."

"A weird coincidence."

"The broadcaster was careful to say that neither victim had ingested any food, and that it appeared the deaths were not related to each other or to the restaurant. Maybe the autopsies will give us some answers."

"Ooh, that's a problem." Darryl groaned. "The Berringers don't want an autopsy."

"They don't want to know how their daughter died?"

"I think they're afraid it was suicide and they'd have to take some of the blame. But I know it wasn't suicide. Kaycie and I used to talk about it and she said she'd never do that to her parents. It was that damn medication that made her crazy. She wasn't like that. Even drowsy, she was in good spirits driving to the brunch, and she talked a lot about the baby. She still called it 'our' baby."

"Could she have accidentally overdosed?"

"Not a chance! She was a health nut. She hated taking pills."

"Still — she was depressed, wasn't she?"

"She liked to feel sorry for herself. And she was bulimic. She'd go on sudden eating binges and then go whoops in the bathroom."

"She was bulimic? Some health nut!"

"I know," said Darryl. "She couldn't see the irony. She thought her purging, as she called it, was cathartic." A long sigh. "Rob and I stopped at the flat on the way home — I still have my key — and we searched the place for a 'goodbye' note. There wasn't any. The only thing unusual was a wet tea bag and one of those little Splenda wrappers in the kitchen sink. Kaycie only drank coffee. And she had a thing about artificial sweeteners. She wouldn't go near them. Needless to say, we didn't touch a thing."

"You think she had a visitor?" asked Hallie.

"I don't know. She didn't have a lot of friends."

"Enemies?"

"She mentioned a loony customer who threatened her."

"Hmmm." Hallie thought a moment. "I'd like to take a look at the flat before her parents get there. Maybe tonight."

"Good idea. They aren't going over till tomorrow. I left the key under the doormat. But you shouldn't go alone. Will Cas go with you?"

"No, his magazine, *Citytalk*, is having their annual holiday dinner. I'd better get moving — oh, do me a favor? Call Dr. Toy at the coroner's office and leave word that the police are investigating the deaths, and under no circumstances should he let anyone pick up either body. Okay?"

"Will do. Be careful, Hallie."

— **Chapter 46** —

AWARE that she was invading a possible crime scene, Hallie found the key and entered Kaycie's flat silently. Caution told her not to turn on lights. A nosy neighbor might have heard the news and wonder who was snooping around.

Armed with gloves, plastic bags, tape, a can of Luminol to detect blood, a camera and a flashlight, she started in the kitchen. To her relief, the spray revealed no blood. After dropping the tea bag and Splenda wrapper into plastic bags, she checked the dishwasher. Strange. Dirty dishes, but no glass or teacup. Whoever drank the tea would have washed the cup and put it away. Pressing her tape on the faucet handle, she hoped to collect a fingerprint or two. Everywhere she went, she snapped pictures.

Next, she ventured into Kaycie's bedroom. Clothes were strewn about; she must have had trouble deciding what to wear. The bed was unmade. No signs of a struggle or anything unusual. Atop the dresser, untouched, sat Kaycie's purse with her wallet and credit cards. She hadn't taken it to the brunch. Hallie left it there, next to a photo of Kaycie and Darryl laughing, with arms entwined.

The bathroom was equally messy; towels on the floor, throw rugs full of spots. Hallie bagged a nearly-full pill container labeled: "Prozac, 10 mg. Take twice a day with or without food."

Inside the medicine cabinet, she found an impressive collection of vitamins and supplements, plus laxatives and antihistamines. Another shelf held "natural" skin creams, lotions, and hair spray. A peek into the second bedroom, where Darryl had slept, gave her a start. It was pristine — almost a shrine. It looked as if nothing had been touched since she left.

The living room smelled stale and unloved. Couch pillows were puffed as if they hadn't been sat on in ages. Hallie ran her gloved finger over a side table and got dust. Looking closer, she noticed a dust-free circle, the size of a saucer, where something that had been there for a long time was removed — probably recently, since no new dust had time to collect. Could Darryl have taken something? But she said she hadn't even gone into the living room.

As Hallie was checking her camera, a noise startled

her. Someone was turning a key in the front door!

Dousing her flashlight, she grabbed a fireplace iron and crouched behind a sofa. The door opened...footsteps...lights...and she could see a woman striding down the hall. A print caftan engulfed a short figure. Hennaed red hair marked her as possibly Russian.

Hallie emerged on tiptoe, followed her for a few seconds, then took loud steps as the woman turned into Kaycie's room.

She spun around in surprise. "Who you?"

"I'm Darryl's sister-in-law and Kaycie's friend. I've come to collect some of their things."

The woman frowned. "Darl move out. Kaysha die. This my house!"

"You're the landlord? Er — landlady?"

"Wot you tink?" Her hands dropped to her hips. "I Goshenka. You go way!"

Hallie thought quickly. "I work with the police. You know, po—lice? You no touch anything. Fingerprints, understand?" She pointed to her fingertips, then waggled them warningly. "You — no touch!"

"Okay. Okay. You go home? Tell police I no touch nothing. Okay?"

"Okay." Hallie nodded. "You go home, too?"

"My house — there." She pointed south.

"You live next door?"

"Ya, ya."

"Were you here this morning? You drink tea with Kaycie?"

"I no here. This morning I go doctor." She raised

her skirt to show a bandage on her leg. "I go now. Goo'bye."

With a quick wave, she turned and strode out the front door.

— **Chapter 47** —

ONCE MME. GOSHENKA had departed, Hallie left the lights on and went over the rooms again, taking more pictures, but not seeing anything suspicious. A wet tea bag, a Splenda wrapper and an empty space on a table were not great clues. She thought of calling the police to designate the site a crime scene, but how could she prove there was a crime?

After packing up the meager evidence, Hallie drove to her apartment. Cas was staying there while they waited to hear about the house they'd bid on, but he wasn't back from dinner yet.

She checked the clock: nine-thirty p.m., and she was exhausted. He'd be home soon; no reason to wait up. At midnight, however, she woke with a start. No Cas sleeping next to her! Where could he be? It was just *Citytalk's* annual holiday dinner, not a big deal. As executive editor, he hosted it every year in place of the publisher, Ted Attavino, who was always off traveling. Secretly, she was glad that the magazine's budget didn't allow staffers to bring partners or spouses. Business dinners were soooo boring.

By one a.m., Hallie was starting to worry. Cas hadn't had a drink since his AA days. Could he have fallen off the wagon? He'd sneak a cigarette now and then, but she'd almost always smell it and scold him. He once told her she should join the Police Canine Corps; her sniffer was as good as any trained dog.

What to do? Perhaps she should call the restaurant and find out when the party broke up — or perhaps it was still going on? As she was pondering, noises at the front door made her sit up. A moment later, Cas tiptoed in, carrying his shoes.

"Hi, honey," he smiled. "I didn't want to wake you."

"Where've you been?" she demanded.

He stared at her. "You know where I've been. The same place I've been for the same event for the last three years. What's the big deal? Why'd you wait up?"

"I thought you'd be home early. I was worried."

"Sorry about that. It went on later than I expected."

He set down his shoes and moved to embrace her. She froze and stepped back.

"What the hell's going on, Hal? What are you mad about?"

She took a step closer. "You stink of perfume. And you've got lipstick on your face!"

"Yeah, big frickin' deal. One of our interns kissed me on the cheek. For God's sake, Hal, can't you quit sleuthing for five minutes? We haven't even been married two days and you're already a jealous wife."

"I am not! It's been a long day and I needed you to be with me, not out flirting with pretty young interns."

"I won't dignify that with an answer." He snatched his pajamas from a drawer. "I'll sleep on the couch."

— Chapter 48 —

CAS LEFT FOR WORK early Monday morning, leaving Hallie a note. "Sorry, honey, I should've called last night. I love you."

She saw it, smiled, and reached for the phone. He answered right away.

"I'm sorry, too," she said. "Remember when you told me I was ninety-five percent angel and five percent bitch?"

"Yes."

"I guess the bitch came out last night."

"She did indeed. Tell her to stay the hell out of our lives, huh?"

"I will, darling. Tell me about last night?"

He reported on the party, who was there, what they discussed, and the fact that the publisher ordered they close the office on Fridays for budget reasons. Salaries would be cut accordingly. A few welcomed a three-day weekend, but most were upset, and inclined to drown the bad news in alcohol. He felt for his employees, hadn't wanted to desert them, and no, he hadn't broken his AA vows.

Then he asked about her evening, and learned of her visit to Kaycie's flat, her brief chat with Mme. Goshenka, and the fact that the Fronds wanted an autopsy, but the Berringers didn't. He offered to go with Hallie to try to convince them otherwise. She'd call to set it up. But first, she would speak to Dr. Toy.

In case she had forgotten, although she hadn't, the Medical

Examiner reminded Hallie that they'd met some years prior, when she was promoting a No Smoking campaign for the city. He greeted her politely on the phone, and yes, he'd have time to answer her questions…if he could.

"For starters, Dr. Toy, may parents refuse to have an autopsy performed on their daughter for religious reasons?"

"I believe you're referring to the young woman we found yesterday," he said, assuming a professional tone. "Since her death was unexpected and unexplained, and the circumstances surrounding it are undetermined, the answer is no. The parents do not have the last word. We perform autopsies to answer questions in the public interest. This is how we find out about epidemics and diseases, not to mention homicides."

"Ah, good." Hallie sighed with relief. "Kaycie was mildly depressed and took Prozac, but her ex-housemate, my sister-in-law, is sure she didn't commit suicide. We think it could have been accidental — or otherwise."

"Otherwise?"

"Anything's possible. How soon can we get a report?"

"Patience, young lady. We must first establish the cause of her death — whether it was a pre-existing medical condition, an injury, or a form of poison, such as alcohol, drugs, toxic substances. We have to document any internal or external injuries, collect tissue biopsies and body fluids, and do a toxicology screen. All this takes time. The earliest we could finish a report would be four weeks, if there are no complications."

"What kind of complications?"

"There may be a need for tests other than the panel of drugs in a routine autopsy. Perhaps your sister-in-law can tell us what medications Kaycie took besides Prozac. The toxicology report will determine whether there were lethal levels of any drugs in her system when she died."

"Why does it take so long?"

"We believe every death is as important as every life. We don't bump people because someone is more famous, or some ambitious journalist wants an exclusive. If you want to pay four or five thousand dollars, you can hire a private pathologist with access to a toxicology lab. He could complete an autopsy and tox screen in a week or less."

"The family would never agree to that even if they could afford it. Don't you ever put a 'rush' on a case?"

"Can you tell me why I should?"

"Aren't there poisons that show up at first, but not later?"

"Yes. There are also poisons that don't show up at first, but appear later. There was a case where a young law student died suddenly a few years ago. His death was ruled due to cardiac arrhythmia and his wife donated his tissues and organs to research, then had his body cremated. A year later, scientists found high levels of arsenic in his tissues — more than a thousand times the normal level in his liver and more than two hundred times the acceptable level in his kidneys. The wife went to prison for murder. So you see, rushing an autopsy isn't always wise."

"I guess not," she murmured, "and I assume getting closure for the family isn't reason enough to hurry it."

"You assume right," he answered. "I'll send copies

of the report to the police." And he was gone.

— Chapter 49 —

HALLIE LOST NO TIME phoning Paul Dodson. "Sorry," said his assistant. "Judge Dodson is in chambers."

"What exactly does that mean?" she asked.

"He's hearing a case in a private room, not in open court. What's the nature of your inquiry?"

None of your business, she thought, but maybe his job was to screen calls. "I'm a friend. I'd like him to ask the coroner to give priority to two autopsies."

"Is there an emergency?"

"Not exactly."

"Then write a letter," said the assistant, and hung up.

Still in her robe and nightgown, Hallie checked the clock: ten past ten. Today was Mumsy's hip replacement surgery, and Hallie was driving her to the hospital at eleven. Dressing quickly, she hurried to the house and found her mother in good spirits, hoping the operation would end her chronic pain.

A few hours later, Edith Marsh was wheeled into the Operating Room, and Rob joined Hallie in the waiting area.

"Sorry Darryl couldn't come," he said, kissing his sister's cheek. "She has a show today and sends her good wishes."

"Thanks. How are things going with you two?"

"Dicey. I'm crazy in love with her, but she can't seem to let go of Kaycie. She's determined to help you find out why she died, and it's driven a wedge between us. That damn woman tried to kill me!"

"I know. Don't ever tell Mumsy. In a way, you have to admire Darryl's loyalty. She knows Kaycie's good qualities, and she's sure that her hostile behavior was a side effect of her medication. She's also sure that Kaycie didn't commit suicide."

"Frankly, I don't give a shit. I'm glad Kaycie's gone. She would've been nothing but trouble to Darryl and me — and especially to our baby."

"Shhh! Don't say that to anyone. It gives you a motive."

"Motive? Me? You think I killed her?"

"Don't be stupid, Robbie. But I am taking all this to the police. I'm pretty sure I can make a case for possible foul play, or maybe medical neglect, as soon as I get the autopsy report. In the meantime, I want to visit her parents and find out all I can about her background."

"Ah, the sleuth strikes again! Don't you ever get tired of snooping into people's lives?"

"No. And thanks for reminding me. I'm calling the Berringers right now."

— **Chapter 50** —

IT WAS EARLY EVENING before Edith Marsh was wheeled out of the recovery room and returned to her hospital bed. The doctor informed Hallie and Rob that the surgery was successful. If all went as planned, the patient could go home in three days. In the meantime, a private nurse would stay with her 'round the clock.

Edith opened her eyes long enough to reassure her children that the pain was bearable, then fell back asleep. Rob went off to a gig in the East Bay; Hallie had talked the Berringers into letting her and Cas come by at seven. At first, Charlotte Berringer said they weren't seeing anyone, especially not a friend of Darryl's, whom they still blamed for their daughter's death.

Hallie had sympathized, but thought they might want more information about the circumstances, and how Kaycie, even though she wasn't feeling well, hadn't wanted to disappoint her good friend. Hallie added that, "Everyone who knew Kaycie loved her" — a statement she would have no way of knowing. But it worked.

Charlotte and George Berringer lived in the Sunset District, not far from Ocean Beach, and as Charlotte proudly explained, "Three doors down from our church." A few minutes past seven, she met Hallie and Cas at the front door, and ushered them into a small, cozy living room.

The house was modest, the furniture basic and boring. A vase of fresh-cut flowers and a plaster Jesus decorated an upright piano. An oversized TV sat on a makeshift wooden table next to a stack of magazines, some still in cellophane. The fireplace appeared dusty and unused. Well-scrubbed carpet stains confirmed the presence of their Bernese Mountain Dog, asleep by the couch.

Devoid of makeup, Charlotte looked to be a well-preserved seventy, slightly overweight in her purple sweats. A gold cross dangled on a chain around her neck. Gray hair tied back in a bun, a wrinkled forehead, and wide amber eyes full of questions gave her an aura of innocence. Her voice was soft and sad. "Come in, please. Have a seat."

Seconds later, George Berringer appeared, a short, bald man with an angry frown. His long-sleeved "Go Giants!" T-shirt covered a bulky frame. He shook hands reluctantly, sat down opposite his guests and folded his arms. "Why are you here?" were his first words.

"We're very sorry for your loss," Hallie said, knowing how empty that sounded. "Your daughter was a wonderful person."

"Oh, she was," said Charlotte, her voice cracking. "She was always thinking of others, even as a youngster…"

She droned on, telling story after story of their only child, spilling out her heartbreak. Her rambling left no opening for questions. In the midst of a seemingly non-stop monologue, Cas gave Hallie a raised eyebrow. She responded with a barely perceptible nod.

"Mrs. Berringer," he said, "Excuse the interruption. Your tales are wonderful, but I'm wondering if I might trouble you for a glass of water. For some reason, I'm —"

"Oh, forgive me," she said, getting up, "I'm a terrible hostess."

"I'll help you," Cas offered, following her into the kitchen.

Alone with Kaycie's father, Hallie quickly turned to him. "Why are you so hostile to Darryl, Mr. Berringer? She was a good friend to your daughter. Kaycie loved her."

"You call that love? She was a goddamn pervert," he growled. "Don't tell me you don't know that she and Kaycie were lovers. She seduced my little girl."

"I happen to know that's not true. They loved each other but not the way you're thinking."

"Cut the crap, lady, I've been around the block. I've seen these homo types and I know what they do. Kaycie even told us she wanted to marry Darryl. She said Darryl got herself pregnant so they could have a baby. She thought we'd be thrilled to know we were going to be grandparents. Grandparents! They don't even know who the father is! Exactly what were we supposed to tell the rest of the family? Our neighbors? Our minister?"

"Maybe Kaycie *thought* it was 'her' baby, but it wasn't, Mr. Berringer. And we do know the father. Darryl and my brother Rob are in love, and she accidentally got pregnant. It wasn't until Darryl decided to move out of their flat that she learned of Kaycie's strong attachment to her."

"Bullshit! Kaycie was a good daughter until Darryl corrupted her. She got furious at us when we told her we didn't approve of her affair — said she and Darryl would be together forever. I told her that was sick, and that if she continued the relationship, she wasn't my daughter any more. When Darryl dumped her for the rich guy —"

"My brother."

"When Darryl dumped Kaycie, it literally killed her. The bitch broke her heart! I don't need any damn autopsy to tell me why my daughter died."

Hallie wasn't about to inform him that he had no

say about an autopsy. "A last question, Mr. Berringer, if you don't mind. I heard something about a man harassing Kaycie at your flower shop. Do you know about that?"

He nodded. "Yeah. Last Thanksgiving, this big tough-looking guy comes in and buys a holiday special — a white phalaenopsis in a porcelain pot. All for thirty bucks. Helluva buy. He pays cash. Comes back three weeks later, brings in the plant, and the poor thing is dead. Not only is it over-watered, I can see in two seconds that it didn't get enough light. Everyone knows you don't put an orchid plant in a north window. So this big thug starts yelling at Kaycie and demands a refund."

Hallie nodded.

"Kaycie could be tough when she wanted to be. She starts yelling back at the guy and the next thing I know, she's punching him in the stomach! He swats her away like an annoying mosquito, makes an obscene gesture, disappears, and comes back later with his wife. They threaten to call the cops but never do. Kaycie insists the guy hit her first and it was self-defense. I don't know. I didn't see how it started. The wife finally gets the guy to go home. He never presses charges, but for the next two weeks, he's screaming on the phone in a drunken rage, and sending threatening letters. Then suddenly, it all stopped."

"Do you have the letters?"

"Yeah, every other word is either obscene or misspelled. They're somewhere in the shop. "

"Could I see them?"

"What for? Kaycie's gone and our minister says we have to move on. God's will is God's will. The Lord knew

Kaycie was in a bad emotional state and would never be happy again. He wanted to spare her the pain of losing someone she thought she loved. His taking her was an act of mercy. I tell Charlotte we have to be grateful —"

At that moment, Cas returned with a glass of water. He pretended to be thirsty and finished in a few gulps. They sat politely for five minutes, then Hallie glanced at her watch and signaled Cas. They offered condolences, thanked their hosts and left.

— Chapter 51 —

"BRILLIANT!" said Hallie, as soon as she and Cas were in the car, driving home. "How clever of you to leave me alone with Mr. B. He told me exactly what I wanted to know."

"And that is…?"

"Remember Darryl mentioned some tough guy was hassling Kaycie? I didn't dare ask for his name, but I learned that his letters are in the flower shop. He wouldn't give them to me, so we'll have to get them."

"And how do you plan to do that?"

"I don't know yet." She smiled. "But we will. Did you learn anything from Mrs. B.?"

"Matter of fact I did. Mr. B. has obviously convinced his wife that Kaycie's death was a good thing — what'd she call it? Oh, yes, an act of mercy. He told her Kaycie would never have been at peace with herself. Losing her was a horrible shock to them, but now they pray to God and thank Him for saving her and sparing her a lifetime of grief."

Hallie pondered a minute. Then she said, "Mr. B. gave me that line, too. Are you thinking what I'm thinking?"

"That maybe papa B. was the one who done her in?"

"He had opportunity. She worked with him every day. He had motive. Kaycie told them they were going to be grandparents of her and Darryl's baby. His big concern was what they'd tell their neighbors and their minister."

"So maybe he snuck a dollop of arsenic in her water bottle?"

"Maybe. It's available, cheap, virtually tasteless and odorless. But I want to talk to the letter-writer before we go any farther. Could we break into the flower shop on the way home?"

"We could," he said, slowing for a stop signal, "but I have better plans for this evening."

"Do they include me?" She snuggled up to him.

He laughed and kissed her forehead. "Only if you feed me first."

— Chapter 52 —

HALLIE SPENT the next two mornings casing "Berringer's Blooms," a colorful flower shop on Ocean Avenue, and within walking distance from the owners' home. Next door was a consignment store, and Hallie brought in two cashmere sweaters to sell, so she could chat with the woman in charge.

George Berringer, she learned, ran the flower shop. His wife sometimes worked there, but hadn't been in since their tragedy. An assistant named Gary helped out and was always there at noon, when the boss went to lunch with a friend.

Hallie's plan was simple. She couldn't use Cas; the Berringers would recognize his description if they heard it. They'd never met Rob, however, and he was still the all-American boy, complete with corn-yellow hair and a splash of freckles across his nose. Cute, she knew, and the picture of innocence.

Rob was happy to help — "Anything for Darryl, even breaking the law" — although Hallie insisted the plan was foolproof, with only a teeny touch of larceny.

At twelve-ten on Thursday, Rob entered Berringer's Blooms. A slim man of about fifty was quick to offer help. "A birthday gift? Yessir! We've got everything you could possibly want and then some. Roses are a bit common, don't you think? My name's Gary. And you are?"

"Robert."

"Nice to meet you, Robert. May I ask your price range?"

"Fifty — maybe seventy five," said Rob. "I want something unusual – something to knock her eyes out."

No, a lovely flower arrangement didn't appeal to him. It had to be a gift that would last. They finally found what Gary described as "An extraordinary combination of shade plants, fresh from the wilds of China and Tibet."

"How much?" asked Rob.

"A bit more than you want to spend, but worth every cent. It's $89.99. May I point out to you the rare cisporum canoniense Night Heron? Also, this —"

"I'll take it." Rob handed him a hundred dollar bill.

"You won't be sorry."

As Gary began to write up the transaction, Hallie, in a dark wig, sweater, jeans and sneakers, wandered in and casually looked around. She spotted an open cabinet by the cash register. Not a likely place for letters. Only supplies were visible.

Just beyond, a door marked, "Private — Keep out" had to be the office. She checked her watch, and according to schedule, let out a moan, grabbed hold of Rob, and seemingly fainted in his arms.

"Oh, Lordy," he groaned. "Gary, your customer just passed out! Can you — oh, wait, she's coming to. Are you okay, Miss?"

"I'm terribly sorry," Hallie said, in a weak voice. "I — I had minor surgery yesterday. Could I possibly lie down for a moment?"

Gary was right there. "Yes, indeed! Are you sure we can't call an ambulance?"

"No, thanks. If I could —"

"Come with me." Taking her arm, Gary led her into the back office and over to a couch. "The boss likes to nap here. Make yourself comfortable."

"Thank you. Just a few minutes, I promise, then I'll be out of your hair."

"Take your time. I have to finish with a customer."

No sooner had Gary shut the door, than Hallie was off the couch, tiptoeing to the desk. The drawers contained noth-

111

ing unusual. A long, messy table with dead leaves, flowers and branches caught her eye, then Bingo! Next to them sat a box labeled "Complaints." She flipped it open and spotted a stack of letters tied with a rubber band. They were addressed to Kaycie, and someone had scrawled "Nut Case!" across the top envelope.

A glance told her they were what she wanted. She chose two letters from the middle, and dropped them into her purse. Enough were left so that unless Mr. Berringer had counted them, which she doubted, they would not be missed.

Mussing her hair and wiping off her lipstick to look pale, she straightened the pillows on the couch and walked out of the office.

"I feel much better now," she said, slipping Gary a ten dollar bill. "Thanks for your trouble."

PART 9

Chapter 53

HALLIE HAD NOW collected two threatening letters signed by a man named Max Winchill, a teabag, a Splenda wrapper, a container of Prozac pills, and a slew of pictures, including one of a dust-free spot on a table. Not too exciting.

The officers who'd come to the restaurant after the two deaths would have filed their report, and sent it, at Cas's request, to his ex-girlfriend, Police Lieutenant Helen Kaiser.

Hallie had worked with Helen before, and liked her. Tough and exacting, she was also known for being detail-oriented, honest and fair. She and Cas had been lovers in the early years of their careers, when Cas was Bureau Chief for the Associated Press in Washington, and Helen was a reporter. His drinking, he later admitted, broke them up. Not until he fell in love with Hallie, in fact, had he seriously stuck to his AA vows.

He'd told Hallie all about the affair. A few months after they'd ended it, Helen had surprised everyone by leaving the news business to attend the police academy. Despite warnings, teasing, even ridicule from her fellow journalists, she graduated from the academy, joined the force, proved herself worthy of constant promotions, and today, Lieutenant Kaiser was rumored to be a future Chief.

Rather than bother Cas, Hallie made the call to Helen herself. A day later, she heard back.

"I've read the police report and seen your photos of the young woman's residence," Helen said. "I'm not convinced we're dealing with paired homicides. From what you told the police, the doctor could've died from natural causes and the woman on antidepressants was probably a suicide."

"Darryl, my sister-in-law, and Kaycie, the female victim, were close friends," Hallie answered. "She's positive Kaycie didn't kill herself. And Dr. Frond, I hear, had tons of enemies."

"I remain unconvinced. But since it's you, Hallie, and your gut instincts are usually on target, we'll take a look pending the autopsy reports. Have you found anything linking the two deaths? Have you looked for a connection?"

"Till my eyes cross over, and I'm still looking. There may not be one, other than that the two victims were at the same place at the same time. They didn't know each other, had no business dealings, traveled in different social circles, went to different churches, yet Darryl insists Kaycie would never take her own life or overmedicate herself."

"So you tell me."

"I understand your skepticism. Cas thinks I'm taking a button and sewing a suit around it. But some things just don't add up. And I'm grateful you're willing to look at the evidence."

"For God's sake, Hallie, you haven't got any evidence! I know you like to solve mysteries, but where's the crime in a wet teabag? On the other hand, you deserve at least a hearing. I'm assigning your 'case' to our best homicide detective, Theodore Baer, better known as Teddy Bear."

"You're giving me a detective named Teddy Bear?"

"It's a nickname, and he fits it. Big and strong with a soft heart, but he's as tough and sharp as they come. The problem is he's also got a heavy caseload."

"You know what they say about busy people. We're the guys who get things done."

"Okay, then. I'll have him call you Monday. Have a good weekend and best wishes on your marriage. Cas is one lucky bastard."

— Chapter 54 —

ROB HAD BEEN ANXIOUS to see Darryl and report on their success at the flower shop, but she'd had to work Thursday night, so they met for dinner Friday.

This situation is weird as hell, thought Rob, knocking on her apartment door. How'd he let himself be talked into such a frustrating arrangement? You were either married or you weren't. Still, he reminded himself that the baby was mainly his fault, and that whatever happened, his son or daughter would have two parents who loved him — or her.

Yet when Darryl opened the door, breathtakingly beautiful in a pale blue silk blouse and slacks, his resentments suddenly vanished. He called on all his will power to keep from taking her in his arms.

"So you're my blind date," he said, hoping he covered his feelings. "Are you going around with anyone?"

"I'm not sure," she said, smiling, "but I think I got married a week ago."

"Then why aren't you living with the guy? He's probably nuts about you."

She laughed and ignored the question. "I'm ready to go. I'll get my coat and purse."

Dinner at The Big Four restaurant started out well. Darryl had been a hostess at the Auto Show the night be-

116

fore, and was eager to describe the "glacier blue" Tesla Roadster on display.

"It takes 3.7 seconds to get up to 60 mph, and each charge is good for 245 miles," she reported. "There's zero tailpipe emissions or pollution. Electric cars are the cars of the future."

"You sound like a fucking commercial. What does the car cost?"

"Over a hundred thousand. We weren't supposed to talk about costs. If we thought someone was interested, we'd send them over to the sales person."

"Damnit, Darryl, I hate your doing stuff like that. It's beneath you. You're my wife now, whether you like it or not. I can support you and I will. I don't expect you to take my name unless you want to. But I'm glad you're wearing your wedding ring."

"I'm glad I wear it, too. It saves me from the creeps. And I appreciate your offer to support me. I've stopped taking new jobs, I'm just honoring the commitments I had. When I start to show in my clothes, Hallie's putting me to work in her office. I'm pretty sure I'll be able to live on my savings and whatever she pays me."

"My sister hired you? Without telling me? What would you do?" He didn't wait for an answer. "It doesn't matter. Why would you work while you're pregnant? You need to stay home and take care of yourself."

His reaction astonished her. "What century are you living in, Rob? Women today work right up to the last minute. Some even have their babies on the job."

"Not my wife and my baby! Okay, so I'm square.

I'm not cool. I love my sister, but your livelihood is my business, not hers. Besides, she's a bad influence. Is she still convinced Kaycie didn't kill herself?"

"I'm still convinced. And she's helping me find out the truth." Darryl frowned. "Didn't you once tell me I was free to be myself? Aren't you the young man who left town because his mother treated him like a possession? Has it occurred to you that I might not want to be treated like a possession?"

She reached for her coat. "Maybe this dinner wasn't a good idea. I'll catch a cab…"

"Like hell you will! I'll take you home." He motioned to the waiter and handed him a bill. "Sorry we can't stay. We'll come back another night — maybe."

Chapter 55

ROB WAS STILL FUMING when he arrived at his own apartment. Neither he nor Darryl had said a word in the car. When he walked her to her door, she uttered a quick "Goodnight," and disappeared.

Hallie was at home to get her brother's angry call. "Sure, I said I'd hire Darryl," she told him. "My assistant, Ken, is taking off for six months. Darryl can fill in while he's gone. And if she has the baby at work, so what? I can snip an umbilical cord."

"Not funny. Why does she have to work? Can't she just be a normal woman and let me support her?"

"Normal women like to work, Rob. They need to use their brains and whatever skills they have. Darryl is a

118

bright, beautiful woman who knows how to meet and talk to people. She'll be a wonderful help to me. And I admire her independence. Your marriage is on probation; no one knows where it's going, so she doesn't want you supporting her. I respect that."

"You girls all stick together," he said, somewhat appeased.

"I'm not a girl. I was going to call you. I need you again."

"Oh, no," he groaned. "What now?"

"You and I are going to pay a bereavement call on Leah Frond. Mumsy can't go and she wants us to do the honors."

"Are you planning to interrogate the poor woman? Do you think Dr. Frond was murdered, too?"

"I don't know. I just think two unexplained deaths deserve looking into. Maybe when we get the M.E.'s reports we won't have to bother. In the meantime, no, I won't ask about her husband's enemies. But you're friendly with Egan. He saw his father die in strange circumstances. Couldn't you ask him to let me peek at his files? Maybe a calendar or a datebook?"

"He'll want to know why."

"Tell the truth. Tell him we don't want to upset his mother. Please, Robbie, I really need you to go with me and talk to Egan in private, if he's around. I heard he was staying with his mother this week."

"My name's not Robbie!" His voice softened. "You know I can never say no to you. When do you want to go?"

"Tomorrow's Saturday. Are you free Sunday?"

119

"I was hoping to be with Darryl, but that doesn't look too promising. So yes, unless I get a gig."

"Good. I'll let you know when to pick me up."

— Chapter 56 —

HOME ALONE later that evening, Rob began to berate himself. His sister was right, of course. She usually was. He'd been insensitive, to put it kindly, and a thoughtless boor, to be realistic. Darryl had specifically told him she didn't want to be a trophy wife, and that was the last thing he wanted, too. But she was so darn beautiful, how could he not be proud of her? And couldn't he be excused for being a wee bit jealous?

"Get over it, dickhead," he told himself. Yet why, he wondered, did she have to be so stubborn? Or was he the one being stubborn? She obviously wasn't after his money, or she'd have jumped at his offer of support. And why had he expected her to overflow with gratitude at his gross, impulsive, off-the-wall proposal?

Hallie definitely was right. A woman like Darryl needed to be courted, even pampered. She might have responded to a basket of flowers, a letter of endearment, poetry, words of tenderness — anything to make her feel she was as special as she was. Damn it, he thought, I screwed up big time.

Yet there was hope. He must change tactics completely. From now on he would think before he spoke or acted. He would never again question her desire to work or be independent. He would "handle with care" the woman he loved, as if she were a delicate jewel. Above all, he would encourage her to be herself and not have to live up to anyone's expectations but her own.

He checked his watch; it was getting late. Time to stop beating up on himself and moping around like a lovesick teenager. He would send flowers in the morning — not a big, expensive, showy arrangement, just a single long-stemmed rose. And the note that went with it would have three short words.

— Chapter 57 —

BEFORE HALLIE AND ROB made their Sunday call, Hallie took time to read Dr. Gerald Frond's flattering obituary, and do some research. What stood out along with his many medical accomplishments were a number of patented surgical instruments he invented, and his book, "Fakes, Frauds, and Fables," published a year prior, in January of 2010.

"The purpose of this book," he'd written in the Introduction, *"is to enlighten and educate the average person who sees his or her 'spiritual advisor' as a gifted friend and healer, rather than a clever opportunist who preys on the weak and gullible.*

"I have seen too many of my patients get intoxicated by what their 'clairvoyants' tell them. Some have serious ailments. They would rather believe good news from their psychic than the truth from their doctor. Some have died needlessly; some have committed suicide after learning that their 'spiritual guide's' predictions bore no resemblance to reality. While certain individuals may have a keen sense of intuition, long years

of research and experience have shown that there is no such thing as a 'real' psychic who can read the past, communicate with the dead, interpret the present, or foretell the future."

More than a dozen lawsuits followed the book's publication. Nine were dismissed without a hearing. Three caused problems. After eight months, and six-figure lawyer bills, Dr. Frond won two cases and settled the third. One of the losing plaintiffs was Zlotta Kofiszny, a woman who called herself "The World's Leading Celebrity Psychic," and claimed her client list read like a Who's Who of the Rich and Famous. She sounded angry and vindictive, and Hallie thought, of particular interest.

— Chapter 58 —

LEAH FROND LOOKED to be in her late fifties — petite and slim, with short black-and-gray frosted hair. Gold loop earrings framed a once-pretty face, now lined and leathered, probably from hours of sun-baking. Unlike the grieving widow Hallie expected, Leah's eyes were bright and shining, lit up by a smile. A yellow print blouse allowed a glimpse of cleavage, a knee-length skirt showed off shapely legs. Her proud posture conveyed a surprising message.

"I can't mourn Jerry," were her first words as she greeted Hallie and Rob. "I've shed my tears and I'm moving on with my life. Jerry was a fine doctor and a brilliant man, but we had our problems, like everyone else. Come sit down — how's Edith?"

Hallie and Rob followed their host into a spacious living room. Beige Fortuny-covered chairs and couches surrounded a black granite coffee table. Atop it sat a pair of LLadró porcelains and a dish of cashews. Modern paintings by names most would recognize enhanced the walls. A crystal chandelier added to a sense of taste and luxury.

"Mom's amazing," Hallie replied, as they all sat down. "She went home Thursday. She's off major painkillers and walks around the house. She wanted us to thank you for the gorgeous roses."

"My pleasure. What's the prognosis?"

Rob answered, "Her surgeon said it takes about six months for all the wounds and stuff to heal."

"That was a glowing obituary," Hallie offered, moving on to her own subject. "Your husband's book must have saved people a lot of money."

"Jerry was a non-believer, an atheist and a cynic. That's what made him such a good scientist and surgeon. If something wasn't proven to be true beyond all doubts, he would question it. I disagreed with him about almost everything — politics, raising children, religion — but we learned to keep peace in the family by not discussing our differences."

Rob gave his sister a look of warning. He sensed trouble in the marriage and knew she would jump on it. She did.

"The people the public love and admire aren't always adored by their families," Hallie ventured.

Leah took the bait. "You're so right! That obit made him look like God incarnate. Ironic, isn't it? Since he insisted there was no God. He would even preach his stupid ideas to his patients. One was a man in my church who got

123

so annoyed he switched doctors."

Hallie's ears perked. "Was the man angry?"

Rob interrupted before Leah could answer. "The important thing, Mrs. Frond, is that you're getting on with your life. By the way, is that Egan I hear?"

"Yes, he's upstairs practicing. I didn't know Hallie was bringing you. I'm sure he'd love to see you."

"Thanks, I'll follow the music."

As soon as Rob left the room, Hallie honed in. "That man in your church who switched doctors. Was he angry?"

"He was furious! He said Jerry had no right to lecture his patients. He got some other patients to switch, too. But Jerry didn't care. He had a huge practice. He was the best at what he did. He wasn't about to change his views on anything, for anybody."

"I'm so sorry, Mrs. Frond. It sounds like you had a difficult marriage."

"It got worse with the years — and please call me Leah. But Jerry's gone now and it's bad luck to speak ill of the dead. Tell me about you — and best wishes on your marriage."

"Thanks. I'll tell you in a minute." Emboldened by Rob's absence, she asked, "Hope you don't mind my question, but have you ever suspected foul play in your husband's death?"

She laughed. "Martin, the man who switched doctors, doesn't have the balls to kill anyone. But some of those psychics aren't shedding any tears. Jerry was a difficult man. If you want to know the truth, a lot of people are better off, including his partner."

"His partner?"

"Rich Gilbert, the doctor who's taking over his practice. They never liked each other, but then, Jerry didn't get along with most people. We had a private Memorial ceremony, and we invited Rich, but he didn't come. Told someone he didn't want to be a hypocrite."

Hallie's response was cut short by Rob's reappearance.

"Egan's busy on his flute," he reported, "but we've got a gig together next week."

"That's great" said Hallie. "I was just telling Leah about our — uh, weddings." A quick description of the ceremonies, fifteen minutes of grandchildren talk and pictures, and the callers took their leave.

— Chapter 59 —

LATE MONDAY AFTERNOON, Hallie heard from Detective Theodore "Teddy Bear" Baer. He sounded pleasant, and was slightly confused since Lieutenant Kaiser had shared her doubts that a crime was even committed. TB, as he was called, was tied up at the moment, but would be happy to send her "evidence" to the crime lab "if there's good reason." First, however, he would come by her apartment next Monday to get her story.

In the meantime, he would run a check on the two decedents, as well as Max Winchill, the man who'd sent Kaycie the threatening letters. A few mornings later, he informed Hallie that he'd found a record of a Glock 38 pistol once owned by Kaycie Berringer. The recently fired weapon had been turned in to the police earlier that year, on Sunday, January 2nd, by a "concerned friend" who said the owner was "confused and acting crazy." There was no follow-up.

Dr. Frond was clean, but Max Winchill had quite a rap sheet. Currently, he lived in the Sunset district in a house owned by "Mary Iversen," his common-law wife. A sometimes-construction worker and convicted felon, he'd served time for manslaughter after killing a man while driving drunk. CODIS, the Combined DNA Index System, stored his DNA profile. TB made clear that under no circumstances should she try to see or interview Max Winchill.

With her usual impatience, Hallie shrugged off the detective's warning, found Mary Iversen's address online, confirmed that Cas was flying to L.A. for several days, then phoned Darryl. They made a date to call on Mr. Winchill late Friday afternoon; no need to give him advance notice.

— Chapter 60 —

DARRYL HAD JUST FINISHED a fashion shoot, and hadn't had time to remove her heavy makeup. But she and Hallie looked deliberately laid-back in their jackets and jeans as they drove up to the home of the alleged letter-writer.

The white stucco house was small and square with a triangular roof, typical of the neighborhood. A modern bay window spoke of recent remodeling. Beneath it, on either side of a garage door, leafy hedges needed trimming.

No one answered the first bell; the second brought heavy footsteps and a husky voice yelling, "Who's there?"

"We're working with the police, Mr. Winchill," called Hallie, who'd agreed to do the talking. "We need to ask you a few questions."

A minute of silence, then the door opened. The stench of beer and smoke was almost overpowering.

The man who answered was about five-ten with a protruding belly. Wide shoulders and thick muscles bulged through a stained T-shirt. Reddish-brown hair reached to his shoulders, framing a bushy moustache and beard. His face was flushed. Beady eyes squinted at the callers.

"You cops?" he asked.

"We work with the police," said Hallie. "May we come in?"

"Where's your badge?"

"We're not police. We work with them, and some-times —"

"Sure, ya do." He grinned, took off an imaginary hat and bowed gallantly. "Come into my parlor, pretty ladies. Call me Max. Sorry Mary ain't here t'greetcha."

"Thanks, we can't stay." Hallie reached into her purse and showed him an envelope. "Just want to ask if you sent these letters."

"To that slut in the flow'r shop? Sure I sent 'em! Bitch screwed me out of a C-note! I'll get it back, too! My pal Gus went to see —" He stopped short. "How'd you two workin' girls get my letters?"

"We're not prostitutes, Max. My friend's a model. I

run a public relations business."

He frowned. "Don't play me, sweetlips, I ain't in the mood for games. Why'd ya come here? Keep lyin' and I'll twist your pretty noses right off your pretty faces."

"We're helping Detective TB — uh, they call him Teddy Bear — with a case. He's got a real name but I —"

"Detective Teddy Bear? That's a good one!" He chuckled. "Now I'll tell you why you're here. Gus found my letters at the flow'r shop. He got my dough back from the bitch, then he spent it buyin' you two girls for me. Good ol' Gus, the horny bugger."

Before Hallie could protest, he double-latched the front door. "Come right inta the livin' room, officers!" Still laughing and mumbling to himself, he reached for Darryl's arm. "Let's start with the quiet one...'less you wanna make it a threesome?"

Darryl looked at Hallie in terror.

"Well, okay, Max, you're too smart to fool." Hallie smiled flirtatiously. "Gus did send us to surprise you. But Melanoma's new at this. Aren't you, honey? Best you take me first, and Mel can watch. But I need to use your bathroom."

"Yeah, yeah, that's better. Where'd I put my bottle? You girls want a beer?"

"No, thanks. Don't be nervous, Mel, I'll be right back." Hurrying down the hall, Hallie found a bathroom, entered, locked the door. Ignoring the dirty towels and sink, she opened the medicine cabinet. A quick peek told her the man collected pills — of all shapes and sizes. Nothing caught her eye till she spotted an orange plastic container.

128

The label read: "Sildenafil citrate, 100MG tablets; take one by mouth as needed." Inside, three blue diamond-shaped pills marked "VGR 100" confirmed their identity.

Grasping the pill box, she found her way to the kitchen just as their host was pulling a bottle from the refrigerator.

"You've had a few beers, Maxie," she said, waving the medication at him. "If you want both of us, you've gotta be up to it, if you get my meaning."

"Where'd ya find those?"

"In your bathroom. Your doctor ordered them for you. You want us to tell Gus you're a real man, right?" She opened the container and poured the Viagra pills into her hand. "Unfortunately, you've only got three. Most johns take four or five. But a big, handsome guy like you doesn't need much help. You'll do fine with just three."

"Damn right!" He took the pills and gobbled them down with a beer chaser. "How long we gotta wait?"

"Fifteen minutes. In the meantime, Gus said you could tell us some wild tales." She hurried back to the dingy living room. Darryl, pale as an iceberg, sat on a couch beside a coffee table covered with bottles and dirty ashtrays. Max appeared in the doorway, lit a cigar and leaned against the wall.

"Maxie's gonna tell us how he took care of that slut in the flower shop," said Hallie, sitting down beside Darryl. "Tell us, Max. What were you doing in the flower shop that day?"

He burped loudly and puffed his stogie. "Hell, I can't 'member shit!" Garbled words and obscenities poured out for about ten minutes. Then suddenly, his eyes widened in alarm. He stopped talking mid-sentence, slapped a hand over his mouth, spun around and dashed for the bathroom. "Let's go!" Hallie grabbed Darryl's arm. They released the latch, raced out the door and down the steps. Within seconds, they were locked in the car and driving off.

Tears and black mascara streamed down Darryl's cheeks. "Oh, God," she sobbed. "Oh, God, I thought we were —"

Hallie turned the corner and pulled over to the curb. "Don't cry, it's all over. We're safe now." She couldn't resist a giggle. "You should see your face, Melanoma."

"Don't call me that!" Darryl peered into the car mirror, then relaxed into a smile. "What's wrong with looking like a zebra? I — can't believe how cool you were."

"Maybe I seemed cool, but I was terrified." Hallie reached for her cell phone. "Anyway, Mr. Repulsive won't be bothering anyone tonight. I gave him 300 milligrams of Viagra. Add that to cigar smoke and a barrel of beer — he'll be tossing his guts for hours. I'd better call the police."

— Chapter 61 —

ROB, CAS, and especially TB were furious with Hallie for disobeying orders. After a strong scolding the following Monday, the detective informed her that an ambulance had come quickly and taken Max to the Emergency Room. Had he not had his stomach pumped, he might have died.

Considering her thoughtless and irresponsible behavior, there was no way she could charge Max with attempted rape.

On the other hand, Max could charge her and Darryl with attempted murder, impersonating officers, misrepresenting themselves, and any number of broken laws. Fortunately for the women, however, Max was not likely to make trouble. Since he was still on probation, his associating with Gus Perkins, another felon, could send them both back to prison.

Despite her ill-advised efforts, Hallie hadn't learned anything that would or would not make Max a suspect in Kaycie's death. He'd admitted to writing the letters, and remembered the money he thought the flower shop owed him — twice as much as George Berringer said he'd paid. But Max apparently had no memory for what happened later. And why did the calls and letter-writing suddenly stop after two weeks? Was he angry enough and clever enough to have planned a murder? Could he have had help?

What about Kaycie's Dad? George Berringer swore that no one named "Gus" had come to the shop to reclaim Max's money. Could a father be so angry and embarrassed that he would kill his own daughter? And if so, how had he done it? The puzzles remained.

TB told her he'd take the case because she was a friend of Lieutenant Kaiser's but any more shenanigans, and she was on her own. He would come by her house, pick up whatever evidence she had, make a police report and call on Mr. Winchill, preferably when the man was sober — if such a time existed.

Cas took several days to calm down after hearing of the

Friday fiasco, but by Monday he'd extracted a promise from Hallie that she would consult him before attempting any more interviews.

Rob, determined not to be judgmental or possessive, knew that anger would not help his cause. Instead, he told himself he must show love and understanding, and not try to blame Darryl for taking such a foolish risk. Without sounding bossy, he managed to suggest that she think twice — or even thrice — before letting his bullheaded sister involve her in dangerous situations.

Moved by his caring and tenderness, Darryl was contrite, and apologized for exposing their baby to possible harm. She was "coming around," he felt, and had been much warmer since he sent the rose, but he mustn't push her.

Together, the couple had called on Mumsy, who no longer needed pain medicine and was even walking several blocks with her physical therapist. The Winchill incident was never mentioned, and Mumsy assumed Rob and Darryl were happily enjoying Valentine's Day and each other.

No reason to tell her they went home to their eparate apartments.

— Chapter 62 —

AFTER TAKING ALMOST two weeks' distance from the bungled visit to Max, Hallie was excited to get a call from Dr. Toy in the coroner's office. Five weeks had passed since the double-deaths, and she'd had to force herself to be patient and not pester the man.

"We performed a full autopsy and found nothing in Kaycie Berringer's history that would cause us to believe she committed suicide," the M.E. reported. "Nor were there any indications that she would go into sudden cardiac arrest or respiratory failure. As to cause of death, the autopsy was inconclusive."

"What about the Prozac?"

"Contrary to what some people think, antidepressants don't 'make' people suicidal. The Prozac would simply have opened her mind and allowed her to think about alternatives. Also, her medical records show she'd been taking it for some time, so the level of fluoxetine toxicity we found would not have been lethal. No signs of recreational drug use, except for a rather high level of zolpidem tartrate, a sedative hypnotic drug related to benzodiazepine."

"A sedative?"

"A prescription sleeping pill. You know it as Ambien."

"Funny, I didn't see any in her medicine cabinet."

"It's sold on the street. There was no trauma to the body, except for slight enamel erosion in the upper and lower incisors, and abdominal distention, indicating bulimia nervosa."

"Yes, she was bulimic."

"Her central nervous system showed no serious irregularities. My assistant saw an indication of possible head injury, but the brain weighed 1,324 grams and appeared normal. No lesions in the oral cavity, the mucosa was intact, and the airway was unobstructed."

"Darryl, her former housemate, said Kaycie sometimes smoked when no one was around."

"The lungs were unremarkable. The heart was of normal size and configuration, and as I said, there was no evidence of atherosclerosis. Cherry angiomata, common superficial vascular proliferations —"

"In English, Doctor?"

"Forgive me. The body showed a series of red papules — small red bumps on the skin – benign, but to some, a cosmetic nuisance. These red bumps almost blanketed her abdomen and thighs. Kidneys, urinary system, genitals – all within normal limits. No evidence of sexual activity."

"Oh boy, what happens now?"

"That's up to the family. They can have a funeral, a cremation, or order further toxicological tests."

"They'd never agree to that. Could the police order more tests?"

"If they have sufficient cause."

"Could I, as a concerned friend, order a second autopsy?"

"If you want to pay for it. The question is will it help you find out any more than you already know. In most cases, the second autopsy merely confirms the conclusions of the first. And since the organs are already dissected, the new investigators wouldn't be getting the same pristine blood samples. Save your money, Hallie."

"Do all investigators get blood from the same organs?"

"In general, pathologists take blood samples from the veins that feed directly into the heart — specifically, from the femoral vein in the thigh or the subclavian vein near the shoulders. But this blood isn't always available for a second autopsy, so the pathologist may have to seek blood from body cavities. It's usually pooled blood and fluids from the whole body, and isn't much use for determining COD — cause of death."

"I hear you." She paused a few seconds. "How long do you keep the pristine blood?"

"In a questionable situation like this, we'll keep blood and tissue samples for years."

"Could you possibly hold off calling the family or doing anything till I talk to the detective Friday?"

"I can do that. In the meantime, we'll get started on Dr. Frond."

"Thanks, Dr. Toy, I'm most grateful."

"You're welcome. Goodbye."

— Chapter 63 —

DETECTIVE THEODORE "TB" BAER and his partner, Fred Kowalski, arrived ten minutes late for their meeting at Hallie's apartment. Though she had spoken to TB several times, this was their first face-to-face encounter.

He was indeed "big and strong," as Lieutenant Kaiser had indicated. Easily towering over six feet, TB had a ruddy complexion, and a nose that looked as if it had been squashed and somewhat carelessly rebuilt. His smile was warm and his handshake solid, but his eyes gave him away; they were all business and steely cold.

Fred Kowalski was more of a stereotype. Younger

then TB, he wore his uniform with a swagger and spoke fast, often without thinking. In profile, his sharply-defined features reminded Hallie of a Sherlock Holmes caricature. His handshake was weak and brief.

The officers followed Hallie into her breakfast room where they sat at a round table. TB set down a tape recorder and turned it on. He lost no time.

After identifying place, participants, and other vital information, he continued: "On Sunday morning, January sixteenth, 2011, the San Francisco Police Department learned of two unexpected deaths. According to the incident report, an adult male and female unknown to each other entered the SoleMio restaurant (see floor plan) in apparent good health. At approximately one p.m., in separate parts of the restaurant, both Kaycie Berringer and Dr. Gerald Frond died of unknown causes. The Berringer autopsy report is inconclusive and Dr. Frond's body is still awaiting autopsy. Ms. Hallie Marsh, who was present at the scene, will summarize what happened, and what she knows of the investigation to date."

"Sure." Hallie cleared her throat. "My brother, Rob Marsh, and his friend, Egan Frond, were part of a trio playing for a Sunday Brunch at the restaurant. Both the Marsh family and the Fronds were there to support the musicians.

"Shortly after one o'clock, we heard a woman scream. It was Egan's mother, Leah Frond. Egan's father, Dr. Jerry Frond appeared to be having a heart attack. My husband, Dan Casserly, ran over to help, and someone called 911. The firemen and the ambulance arrived, but they couldn't save the doctor, and he died.

136

"His wife said he'd had no heart problems, and a recent checkup had found him in good health, so his death was sudden and unexplained. But for several reasons, including a book he'd written 'exposing' psychics, fortune tellers, spiritual advisors and so on, he had a score of enemies. Am I going too fast?"

"No. Please continue."

"Okay. The Marsh family gathered around the Fronds, to help them, and as soon as the Medical Examiner, Dr. Toy, sent off the body, we returned to our table. My brother's girlfriend, Darryl, had —"

"Last name?"

"Sorry. Darryl Woods. Anyway, Darryl had brought her friend and former housemate, Kaycie Berringer, to the brunch. Kaysie seemed drowsy, so we left her sleeping when we ran over to help the Fronds. When we came back and tried to wake her, she slipped off her chair and fell to the floor. Dr. Toy came running over and pronounced Kaycie dead. He said she'd been dead about an hour — all the time we thought she was sleeping!"

"The coroner's lucky day — two for the price of one," cracked Detective Kowalski.

TB sent a withering look. "Go on, Ms. Marsh. What makes you think that was a crime scene?"

"Well, Detective Kowalski's right. The M.E. did get two bodies. Kaycie had been on Prozac and Dr. Toy thought her death might be suicide. But Darryl, who used to live with Kaycie, said absolutely not, that Kaycie was looking forward to — um, certain good things, and she would never have taken her life. Kaycie's own father, George

Berringer, mistakenly thought she and Darryl were lesbians. He's an exceedingly religious man, and was fearful that his minister or their friends and family would hear about his 'perverted' daughter. He was extremely angry and perhaps could rationalize that he had God's permission to punish her. Bottom line, I guess, is that Kaycie and Dr. Frond both had enemies.

"You think Kaycie's father would kill her?"

"If we knew for sure it was murder, I'd consider him a suspect."

"We all have enemies," interjected Kowalski. "Anyone who doesn't isn't worth knowing. I'd say we're making mucho fuss over a suicide and a heart attack just because they happened at the same time and place."

"It could well be coincidence," Hallie agreed, "but I was curious, so that night, I went to Kaycie's flat and looked around."

"Even though you thought it might be a crime scene?"

"I didn't think the police would come unless they knew for sure it was a homicide."

"Did you find any items missing or damaged? Signs of a struggle?"

"No, but I found an empty Splenda envelope and a wet tea bag in the kitchen sink."

"Ah, the murder weapons!" exclaimed Kowalski.

TB seemed about to snap at his partner, but restrained himself. "Five minute break," he ordered.

— Chapter 64 —

BACK AT THE TABLE, Hallie noticed a subdued-looking Kowalski, who'd obviously been told that his comments were not amusing.

TB picked up the conversation. "You were saying, Ms. Marsh, that you'd found a sweetener envelope and a wet tea bag."

"Yes. Since Darryl insisted Kaycie drank coffee, not tea, and would never use anything but real sugar, it would appear she had a visitor that morning."

"Dirty dishes?" asked TB.

"In the dishwasher, but not in the sink. Whoever was there probably washed his or her teacup and put it back on the shelf. I did press some tape around the faucet handle to get prints. I also took lots of pictures of the flat, including a dust-free circle on a table top where something had recently been removed."

"Anything else?"

"You already know about the other 'suspect'."

"Tell us, please."

Hallie took a long breath. "Max Winchill bought a plant from Kaycie at the flower shop where she worked. It died, he blamed Kaycie, but she wouldn't give him a refund. They fought — physically — and he left. He came back with his wife, but still couldn't get a refund. He was furious and sent off a series of threatening letters. He also made drunken phone calls to the flower shop for about two weeks, then stopped suddenly. I made the mistake of taking Darryl and going to his house on Friday, I think it was

February eleventh —"

"Despite my stern warnings that he was a convicted felon, and not to contact him."

"Yes." She reddened. "I went against your instructions. It seemed nothing was happening in the case. When we arrived at Winchill's house, he was drunk and thought we were — well, hookers. I managed to give him 300 milligrams of Viagra before he tried to act on his belief. When he began to vomit, we escaped and called the police. Again, if we knew for sure that Kaycie was murdered, he might be a suspect — although probably not smart enough to have pulled off a murder with so few traces."

"Where are we now?"

Hallie smiled. "I'd like to help the police as I've done before. Lieutenant Kaiser will, I think, confirm that I've worked on several unsolved crimes and found details that the police overlooked. Since this may not be a case of murder, much less double murder, and despite my recent lapse of judgment, I would like to explore some avenues on my own. That leaves you free, for the moment, to give priority to your heavy caseload."

"Very thoughtful of you," said a newly-polite Kowalski, checking his watch.

"We can't authorize you to act on our behalf, Ms. Marsh. What you do will be strictly on your own and I cannot stress strongly enough that you stay out of harm's way. Do we understand each other?"

"Absolutely! May I give you a few things for the crime lab?"

"Yes. But unless there proves to be sufficient evidence that a crime or crimes were committed, we may close the file."

"Understood. Dr. Toy is keeping blood and tissue samples in case any new evidence appears.

"Thanks for your cooperation, Ms. Marsh. That ends this report for Friday, February 25th, 2011. Detectives Baer and Kowalski signing off."

— Chapter 65 —

A WEEK LATER, Hallie took a call from TB. The tea bag contained only tea. The sole fingerprints on the Prozac container were Kaycie's, and the pills inside were intact. One print on the Splenda wrap was identified as Kaycie's and one was unknown, meaning it didn't match the prints of anyone in their system. But the unknown print did match one on the faucet. Whoever was there with Kaycie may have turned on the water to wash a teacup.

"Could you tell from the prints if it was a man or a woman?"

"No. Some forensic scientists claim you can establish gender from ridge width and density, but it's not always accurate. We did determine that the prints don't belong to Max Winchill. I called his home and talked to Mary Iversen, his common-law wife, about his probation violation. She said he had a serious stroke about the time he was writing letters and threatening Kaycie, so now you know why they stopped. Apparently he does remember the flower shop incident and his friend Gus, but not much else. I told her I'd have to report the ex-cons' association to the parole board, and I got the feeling she'd be glad to get rid of Winchill. In any case, there are no indications to consider him a suspect."

"What about Kaycie's father? Are his prints in the system?"

"I told you, we found no match."

"If I get you Mr. Berringer's prints, could you check again?"

"Yes, but how —"

"Don't worry. I promise to do it legally and safely."

Hallie kept her word. Rob was called into service to go back to the flower shop when the boss was there, and buy something. He did so, paid cash, and asked George Berringer to put the bill of sale into the bag with the carnations.

After leaving the flowers at Darryl's door, Rob delivered the almost-intact receipt to Hallie. She sealed it in plastic and left it at the police station for TB. A call a week later gave her the news. George Berringer's prints on the sales slip were no match for the prints on Kaycie's faucet. The unknown guest was still unknown.

PART 10

— Chapter 66 —

INVOLVED IN THE FASHION WORLD since she was nineteen, Darryl Woods knew most of the resale shop owners in town, who would call her when a special size four garment came in. Sales persons at Saks and Neiman's would contact her when her favorite designer jackets were at final reduction. She knew the stores where she could bargain with the owners. And she knew which local designers would lend her gowns for newsworthy events, because she wore them so well, she was almost sure society photographer Drew Altizer would snap her.

Up until mid-March, when Darryl began her fourth month of pregnancy and began to "show," she'd been able to model almost everything except tight gowns and swim suits. One evening, during Rob's nightly phone call, she mentioned that she'd done her last fashion show for now, and was about to start shopping for maternity clothes. He offered to escort her, reminding her that it was his baby, too, and he'd love to treat her to some new outfits. At first she protested, but he seemed so sincere and anxious to please, she relented.

The next day, they toured the city's best shops — maternity and otherwise. For the first time in her adult life, she enjoyed the luxury of buying whatever she wanted — at full retail!

Knowing that Rob could well afford the shopping spree, her practical eye lit on beautiful top-designer garments she could wear now, then have altered to wear later.

— Chapter 67 —

ARMED WITH A CLOSET full of stylish new clothes, and fresh from a course to sharpen her computer skills, Darryl felt ready to tackle the chores in Hallie's office. Ken Skurman, Hallie's assistant, had indeed taken off for Europe, promising to be back before the baby's due date in September.

Monday, March twenty-first, Darryl's first day at work, was unusually frantic. It had started out quietly. Hallie gave Darryl a tour of the premises, pointing out the file cabinets, the supply closet, the publicity scrapbooks, and whatever else she might need to know about.

"We get lots of calls," she explained, "because we do so much pro bono work. But we have to do due diligence before we can accept a charity as a client. If their overhead's too high, if they're well-established like the Red Cross, or well-known and supported like the Opera, Ballet, and Symphony, we wouldn't be interested. And they wouldn't be interested in our little firm.

"But if they're local, like St. Anthony's, which feeds the hungry, or Conard House, which helps the mentally ill return to society, or if they've almost anything to do with the homeless, we're there for them. I've left you some forms to send out if you think a cause might be right for us."

The instructions continued until Hallie's cell phone rang as they were about to leave for lunch.

"Miss Hallie?" said a shaky voice. "It's Gretchen, one of your mother's caregivers. We're in an ambulance, taking her to the Emergency Room at UCSF, 505 Parnassus. She has pain and swelling in her leg — the one with the new hip."

"Oh, no! Have you called the doctor?"

"Yes, he's meeting us at the hospital. He thinks it might be a blood clot."

"Is she awake?"

"Yes, she's getting oxygen."

"Thanks, Gretchen, I'll be right there!"

— Chapter 68 —

THE MOMENT Hallie left for the hospital, Darryl locked the door. Alone in the office, and not at all sure what to do next, she sat down at Ken Skurman's desk to gather her thoughts. Rob came to mind. She needed to talk to someone, and he was always supportive. But Hallie would have called him, and he'd be on his way to the Emergency Room. A few of her friends might be willing to chat, but they were busy women with little spare time.

Her thoughts turned to Kaycie, and how she had changed in the last few weeks, from a sweet, loyal friend to a crazy, possessive, would-be lover. Was it the medication that transformed her? Was she really gay? Bisexual? Androgynous? And whatever it was, was she born that way? Or was it simply that she idolized Darryl and hadn't had any boyfriends? Now that she was gone, Darryl would never know the truth — and that saddened her.

She could always call her Dad. But every time she did, Brenda would be right there making comments, and she felt uncomfortable with her listening to him. Still, she adored her father and hadn't talked to him in weeks.

Stewart Woods answered his phone on the second ring. "Dad, how're you doing?" she asked, delighted to hear his voice.

"Spunky as ever, now that I'm talking to my beautiful daughter. I've been thinking about you, but I didn't want to interrupt the honeymoon. How's my grandchild?"

"Kicking already. Must be a boy. I have to wait till I'm twenty weeks along to find out. I'll get an ultrasound in May."

"Is it safe for the baby? What do they do?"

"It's very safe if you don't do it too soon. They just put some goo on your tummy and run a device over it and you see the image on a screen. Everything's fine here, Dad. What's happening with you? Is Brenda there?"

"No, she went shopping — again. Your lovely mother-in-law was kind enough to send us tickets to sit in her box seats at the opera next week. Said she can't go out until her hip heals."

"Edith Marsh sent you her opera tickets? How thoughtful of her!"

"Indeed it was. But you know me, I can take opera or preferably leave it." He chuckled. "Not Brenda. She's in a tizzy. She's been shopping every day for something to wear. Nothing in her closet's good enough. She thinks this is our pass key into San Francisco society."

"I'm afraid she's going to be disappointed. Edith's snooty friends probably won't even talk to you. What does she want with a bunch of old snobs, anyway?"

"God only knows." A long sigh. "How are you feeling?"

"Wonderful! No morning sickness, no problems so far. Today's my first day helping Hallie at her office. She's even paying me."

"I'll bet Rob's proud of you. How is your charming husband?"

"He's great." No need to relate their strange marital situation. "What about you, Dad? You never tell me what's going on with your health."

"Not much to tell. I ride my exercise bike every day, take my vitamins and pills, and thanks to Medicare, I see about half a dozen doctors regularly. I'd like to see more of my favorite daughter, too."

"Remember when I was little and you'd say that? I always used to say, 'But I'm your *only* daughter' — and then we'd giggle."

They chatted for another half hour, laughing and sharing happy memories of Darryl's mother, as they could only do when Brenda wasn't around.

As soon as Darryl hung up, she noticed a flock of email messages had come in, another phone was ringing, and someone was knocking at the door. Suddenly, she found herself in charge of a very busy office.

— Chapter 69 —

BY THE TIME HALLIE got to the hospital, Edith Marsh had been moved from the ER to a private room. Before going in, Hallie spotted the orthopedic surgeon at the nurse's station. "How's my mother?" she asked.

The doctor was reassuring. "Looking good. Blood

clots aren't too unusual with hip replacement surgery. They're a minor problem if they stay in the legs. In rare cases, they dislodge and travel though the heart to the lungs, where they can cause a pulmonary embolism. That's why we're watching her. We'll keep her on IV Heparin and Coumadin."

"Does she need all that medicine? What do they do?"

"Heparin increases the body's anti-coagulating activity. Coumadin thins the blood by reducing the production of proteins that the body needs to form blood clots. You're lucky we have these medications. Some hospitals still use leeches."

Hallie made a face. "Leeches?"

"Leeches suck blood. When they start to feed, their saliva releases chemicals that dilate blood vessels, thin the blood, and deaden the pain of the bite. Some doctors think leeches work better than chemical agents."

"Mumsy hates spiders and crawling things. She'd pass out."

"I wasn't suggesting it. If all goes as it should, she can go home in a few days."

"Is she in pain?"

"Some discomfort."

"May I see her?"

"Yes, but don't wake her if she's sleeping."

Mumsy was not sleeping, and seemed surprisingly optimistic. Hallie sent the caregiver home and canceled the attendants for the next few days. Despite her mother's protestations, she insisted on spending the day there. Then she remembered she had an appointment to see Dr. Richard Gilbert, Dr. Frond's partner, that afternoon. She and Cas had talked the night before, and discussed what questions to ask. Cas knew the situation, and who better to interview the man than a prize-winning journalist? Would he go in her place?

Cas's boss, *Citytalk's* publisher, was in Washington, as usual, and the new issue was already at the printer's. He'd be glad to help.

— Chapter 70 —

AFTER A SHORT VISIT to his mother-in-law's hospital room and a hug for his wife, Cas crossed the street in the UCSF Medical Center to the office building where Jerry Frond had practiced neurosurgery for some forty years.

The door to the Stroke Center showed eight names. A gap near the middle indicated that one name, probably Dr. Frond's, had been removed. "Richard Gilbert, MD, PhD" was just below the empty space.

After a short wait, a woman in blue ushered Cas into Dr. Gilbert's office. "Please have a seat. He'll be right with you."

Nothing unusual about the room, Cas thought, glancing around. An iPad, family pictures, scattered papers and a case history folder sat on a well-worn desk. Windows looked out on neighboring homes and gardens, and a wall by the door held the room's only art work — a detailed drawing of the human brain. Awards and diplomas filled the rest of the space.

"Hello, Mr. Casserly," said a friendly voice.

Cas turned to see a tall African-American man with curly gray-black hair. Protruding ears framed a pleasant face with a closed-lip smile. A pink shirt and matching silk tie poked out from under a crisp white coat. Immaculate as he was, he had what Hallie called "the Doctor look" — tired eyes and a weary, resigned manner. After years of performing the most delicate and difficult surgeries, of seeing patients come and patients go, of having to break sad news to them and their families, the work had taken its toll.

The men shook hands. "Thanks for seeing me, Dr. Gilbert. Hallie was sorry she couldn't make it."

"How's her mother doing?"

"Pretty well, thanks. I'll try not to take too much of your time." He set a tape recorder on the desk. "Do you mind?"

"No. Have a chair." The doctor took a seat. "You want information about Jerry. We were partners for thirty-five years. How may I help you?"

"Before I turn on the recorder, do you miss him?"

"I miss his work. He was the most brilliant surgeon I've ever known or watched. I'm the closest thing to a friend he had. He was abrupt, often rude and tactless with patients. His bedside manner was nonexistent. But patients flocked to him. They knew his reputation and they didn't care about his personality. Whether it was migraines or a malignancy, they wanted the best medical treatment they could get. And he provided it." He paused a moment. "On second thought, don't use that recorder."

"I understand." Cas dropped it in his pocket. "Do you have any questions about the circumstances of his death?"

"What in particular?"

"His wife said he'd had a complete physical checkup a few weeks before he died, and that except for some body odor and perspiration problems, he seemed in good health."

"Leah said that?" He rolled his eyes. "Poor woman. I'm surprised she stayed with him all these years. I hope she's happier now. He was miserable to her, to his children, to just about everyone."

"Including you?"

"I tuned him out long ago. Whatever he said rolled off me, so after awhile he didn't even bother to be rude. I was also his physician. He told me I was the only doctor he trusted."

"You gave him the checkup?"

"Barely a checkup. He let me take his blood pressure. It was high but he refused antihypertensive therapy. My nurse gave him an EKG and said it looked 'scary', but he took the paper with him and wouldn't show me. We did blood, x-rays and other tests, but the results all went to him. I never saw them."

"Did you look in his mouth, listen to his heart, tap his knees and do all the routine things?"

"As much as he'd let me. He wouldn't let me listen to his heart but I know he had angina. Sometimes I'd catch him holding his chest. He said he had pains from all his weight-lifting and muscle-building exercises, but I didn't believe it. Once I saw him place a nitroglycerin tablet under his tongue."

"Would it be logical, then, to assume he died of a heart attack? Or cardiac arrest?"

"He died of SCD — sudden cardiac death. It's not the same as a heart attack. A heart attack is what you treat to avoid SCD."

"What causes a heart attack?"

"Something blocks the heart's blood supply. If that triggers chaotic electrical impulses in the heart, it may stop beating."

"Could angina be the cause?"

"Angina patients are at greater risk for heart attacks, but only the autopsy can answer your questions. Why are you asking? You think someone had a hand in his death?"

"I don't know. It seems odd — two people die unexpectedly in the same place at the same time." Cas paused, hoping his next question wouldn't offend. "I'm told Dr. Frond had enemies."

"We all have enemies, Mr. Casserly. Jerry's patients may not have liked him but they knew his abilities. I feel extremely fortunate to have learned so much from him. He was — in his own way — a genius. And geniuses don't have to be nice to everyone."

"I understand. By the way, those medical tests Dr. Frond wouldn't let you see. Any chance I might look at his computer?"

"He didn't use one. I'll see if I can find the reports in his files. If they're any different from what I've told you, I'll let you know."

"I'd appreciate that." Cas rose and dropped his card on the desk. "Thanks for your time, Dr. Gilbert."

— Chapter 71 —

TWO MORNINGS LATER, Hallie arrived at the hospital room just as the orthopedic surgeon was examining her mother.

"The swelling's gone down," he said, after greeting Hallie. "Blood tests indicate the medication's doing its job. We've discontinued the heparin. You can take her home tomorrow."

"Wonderful! What time can I get her?"

"We'll do a test in the morning. You can pick her up around noon."

"Stop talking about me in the third person!" snapped Edith. "I'm right here, in case you haven't noticed."

"Hi, Mumsy." Hallie laughed and kissed her cheek. "I'll stay this afternoon and come back tomorrow at lunchtime."

"No, you won't stay! I want to relax and I don't want to feel guilty about you sitting there. Would you please send her home, doctor?"

"That's not my bailiwick, Edith. I'm pleased that you're sounding like yourself again. I'll start the paper work for your discharge." He opened the door and disappeared.

Convinced her mother was free of pain and truly had no need of her, Hallie left the hospital and headed for her office. Darryl was thrilled to see her.

"It's a madhouse around here," she groaned. "Half a dozen people have to talk to you right away! And the rest just say it's urgent."

"Glad I'm popular." Hallie set down her belongings and hung her jacket on the coat rack. "Thanks for holding down the fort. No more hospital duty. Mumsy's going home tomorrow, so I'll restart her caregivers."

"I keep forgetting to ask you — how was Cas's interview with Dr. Frond's partner?"

"Perfect! Short and sweet. Apparently the good doctor — Frond, that is — was a pain in the butt. He made everyone around him miserable, including his wife and kids."

"Could his wife have — ?"

"Done the deed? It's a possibility we hadn't thought of. Cas took Frond's lawyer to lunch, presumably to get quotes for a story on the new tax laws. He kept refilling the guy's wine glass, then managed to slip Jerry Frond into the conversation and said he hoped he didn't die intestate. The lawyer laughed, assured him that Frond kept his will very much up to date, and left his wife an eight-figure estate. That's more than ten million! Talk about a motive! Everywhere we look, new suspects spring up."

"Was Cas really writing an article?"

"Sure. Said he got some good tax info." She reached into her purse and drew out a piece of newspaper. "Did you see this story in the morning *Chronicle*?"

Darryl glanced at the clipping. "You're kidding! 'Sex May Trigger Heart Attack'?" (Laughter.) "Is that a warning for you or for me?"

"Neither. We were talking about suspects. Suppose the good doctor was screwing around. Or maybe he had a mistress. The article says sexual activity can double a person's chances of having a heart attack within two hours."

"The woman would have to be pretty desperate. From what you tell me, he was in his sixties, unattractive, devoid of charm and a major prick — but rich."

"Exactly my point," said Hallie. "I'll check the female situation with Egan. Meantime, I'm dying to get the autopsy results. Any word from Dr. Toy?"

"No. But some man said he was returning your call to Madame Lotto or something. I put him on the list I gave you."

"Oh, good! That's Zlotta, the psychic who sued Dr. Frond and lost the case. She threatened him in court. I'm dying to talk to her."

"Got another minute?"

"Sure. What's up? My brother behaving?"

"He's been wonderful. He calls every night and sometimes we chat for hours. I'm not sure he'll like what I'm going to tell you, though."

Hallie perched on the edge of Darryl's desk. "Shoot," she said.

— Chapter 72 —

THE PROBLEM was simple, Darryl explained. Her modeling agency had called with an offer. ShowTime was the Mercedes of maternity shops – stylish, prestigious, expensive. The store was preparing a Fall catalog of original designs and needed a model, preferably in her fifth month.

Posing for ShowTime wasn't as exciting as being hired for Victoria's Secret, but it would still be a boost to her career. The job would entail a week of shoots in different Bay Area locations. The pay was $1,500 a day, plus expenses. Was she interested?

"I can use the money to buy baby furniture," she told Hallie. "But I did promise to help you in your office, and if you need me, I won't do it."

"I don't need you. I can get a temp. But I can't speak for Rob. Do you love my brother?"

Darryl stared in surprise. "I adore him! He's the sweetest man I've ever known. He just has to learn to let me have a life."

"He's talked to me about it and he doesn't want to own you. He's proud of your free spirit. He thinks your ex-husband made you somewhat paranoid about commitment. If you love Rob, start letting him do things for you — like pick out and buy the baby furniture with you."

"I can do that. But I'm scared to tell him about the catalog."

"Then don't just 'tell' him. Sit down and talk it over like two mature beings. I bet anything he'll flex. See where I'm going?"

"Yes — and I hope you're right." She nodded, as if approving her own words. "Thanks, Hal. I bow to superior wisdom."

PART 11

— Chapter 73 —

.

ACCORDING TO HER WEBSITE, Zlotta Wladyslawa Kofiszny came to the U.S. from Poland in 1950. She was fourteen at the time, which, Hallie figured, would make her close to seventy-five. She called herself a "Celebrity Psychic," claimed she had visited Mamie Eisenhower in the White House, predicted Elizabeth Taylor would die that very day (March 23rd), and could read the future in kidney beans.

A man answered the psychic's phone and proceeded to interrogate Hallie. No, she was not a reporter, no, she was not writing a book, no, she was not with the IRS, no, she did not want to speak to anyone in the spirit world. And yes, she had seen Zlotta's website, and would simply like the answer to some questions. And yes, she could pay in advance.

"Madame Zlotta is extremely busy," the man told her. "She'll be taping a show in New York, and another in Chicago. But she can see you here at four p.m. on Friday, April 15th.

"Nothing sooner?"

"Afraid not."

"I'll take it." Hallie had decided against using a pseudonym, and left her name, phone and email information, certain that Mme. Zlotta's assistant would lose no time checking her online.

The following Monday, a woman from Dr. Toy's office called. Hallie learned that the Medical Examiner's mother was seriously ill in China, and he'd had to leave suddenly. He wanted her to know that they'd finished Dr. Frond's autopsy, except for the paper work. He would contact her

159

on his return.

Thanks a bunch, she mumbled, after hanging up.

In the meantime, Darryl reported that Rob had indeed flexed about the catalog, and had even congratulated her. All he asked was to see one of her shoots. They agreed that he would drive her to her locations every day, and on the last day of the job, he'd stay quietly in the background and watch while she worked. When she finished, if she wasn't exhausted, they'd go out and celebrate.

— Chapter 74 —

FRUSTRATED that two possible murders might go unsolved, Hallie had to accept that there was little she could do but await her appointment with Mme. Zlotta, and Dr. Toy's return. TB had called from the police station; they'd found no indication that Max Winchill had anything to do with Kaycie's demise. After a brief parole violation hearing, the court had extended his probation time.

Unfortunately, TB reported, the fingerprints on the Splenda wrapper remained unidentified. He would keep the case open but temporarily inactive.

An email from Egan Frond asked Hallie if he could stop by her office that Friday, April Fool's Day. He had something important to show her and it was no joke.

Promptly at three on Friday afternoon, Egan Frond walked into Hallie's office and greeted Darryl. She offered condolences and asked about his mother.

"She's an amazing woman," he said. "Right now

she's planning to take a world cruise."

"Good for her, she's moving on with her life." Remembering Hallie's impatience with small talk, Darryl motioned toward the door. "You're expected, Egan — go right in."

He greeted Hallie with a double-cheek air-kiss. "I see marriage agrees with you. Any news on my father's autopsy?"

"Still waiting to hear." She smiled, glancing at the package under his arm. "You sure know how to pique a person's curiosity. Have a seat?"

"No, thanks. I can't stay. But I need your promise that this is for your eyes only. I wasn't going to show it to anyone. I was all set to burn it, in fact. Dad was a difficult man to live with, and Mom's a new woman now that he's gone. So I didn't mention it to her. But I know you're working hard to find out why Dad died, and I think this book might shed some light. It's his personal diary."

"Fabulous!" Her eyes opened wide. "Darryl and I read an article that said sex could trigger a heart attack. We were wondering about your Dad."

"You want to know about his love life? Read the diary. You'll get your answer — more than you want to know. At first, he wrote very little about his family or his personal life, and pages and pages about his work. I thought he wanted the book to be published because it's so full of medical terms and experiences. But towards the middle — well, you'll read it. And don't be shocked. Dad wasn't stingy with details."

"I'm a big girl."

"I know. You can keep it over the weekend, but I'd like to pop by and pick it up Monday morning. Can I count on your discretion, and a promise not to discuss the contents with anyone except your husband?"

"Of course you can, Egan. I'm touched that you trust me. I'm not sure what to expect since I never met your Dad. But I promise you, I'll keep my word."

"I know you will." He set the package on her desk, blew a kiss. "See you Monday."

— Chapter 75 —

EXCITED, and burning with curiosity, Hallie asked Darryl to take her calls while she tore open the package. Inside was a leather-bound book, about nine inches long and quite thick. It had a lock, broken, she assumed, when Egan discovered it. The first page of the diary was dated January first, 2010, and continued until January eighth, 2011.

The doctor had started out scribbling patients' names and reminding himself to make hospital visits. Early entries were full of surgery dates and patient notes, many illegible. But the more Hallie studied his writing, the more she was able to decipher it, recognizing his strange ways of forming certain letters and abbreviating words.

By June of 2010, Frond began to assess his own health and his reluctance to see doctors. *"Fate can take me where she will,"* he wrote. *"Damned if I'll trust myself to a bunch of pompous, self-serving nincompoops who cheated their way through medical school."*

He also recorded some personal reminders, such as,

"My ticker sucks. Cut down on cheeseburgers." In late August, his thoughts shifted direction. He wrote of meeting a patient's attractive widow and getting *"my first erection in years."*

From then on, his hormones took over. Obviously smitten, Frond devoted page after page to the *"magnetic, mysterious, irresistible"* Zoe. Their first coupling, described in detail, took place on a rug in his office, after closing hours. Little by little, he became more and more obsessed with the charming widow, yet maddeningly aware of his own serious heart condition. At 61, even though he was two years younger than his mistress, planning for a future together was out of the question.

When erectile dysfunction became a problem, he began researching medications. Unfortunately, *"Neither sildenafil nor tadalafil had any effect."*

Discovering his testosterone level was below normal, he quoted an article he found, claiming that: *"Many studies...confirm that testosterone is important in modulating the central and peripheral regulation of ED. Testosterone deprivation has a strong negative impact on the structure of penile tissues and erectile nerves, which can be prevented by testosterone administration."*

Fully aware that the male sex hormone, touted to increase one's sex drive might do just the reverse, he began injecting himself with the powerful steroid, noting every reaction. Fearful of losing his *"darling Angel Zoe,"* he increased the dosage, until the gynecomastia (growth of breast tissue), aching injection sites, shrunken testicles, and bouts of temper made him stop. Plus, he had no appetite for food, much less sex. The experiment had indeed backfired.

When Zoe complained of his sweating and bad smell, he knew he was acting irrationally, and wrote: *"I had to confide in Rich. I had to explain my lack of control and abusive behavior. Rich found elevated levels of testosterone cypionate in my urine, took me off the steroid regimen, and against my will, put me in a wheelchair and rolled me over to the hospital. I was promptly intubated, and God only knows what he gave me. I fell asleep and woke up not knowing where I was or what happened. Leah was by my bed. She told me I'd picked up a bad virus, but that Rich would send me home if I felt well enough. I can never thank Rich enough. He saved my face, saved my marriage, what was left of it, and probably saved my life."*

Zoe had no use for him after that incident, refused to see him, and sent him into a depression. So much for the sex-may-trigger-heart-attack theory. Dr. Frond couldn't have had sex before the brunch if he'd tried. That was his last mention of Zoe, leading to lengthy reports of angry discussions with Rich who wouldn't let him perform surgery until he regained his health.

"Rich was right," he admitted on the last page. *"I was in no shape, mentally or physically, to operate on the human brain. That was the final blow."*

Since the diary no longer held any interest for him, he stopped writing in it. He died a week later.

— Chapter 76 —

WHEN EGAN CAME BY TO COLLECT the book on Monday,

Hallie asked him if his mother, Leah, knew about Zoe.

"I doubt it," he said. "She's never said anything to me. But I don't think Dad ever got over her. He left her fifty grand in his will — described her as a 'former patient' in need."

"Did you ever meet her?"

"I tried to track her down, out of curiosity, but it seems she took the money and ran. The lawyer thought she moved to Paris."

"And your mother never questioned the bequest?"

"Mom didn't pay much attention. What's fifty grand when you're getting millions? Dad left Mom his practice, his book royalties and the profits from all the surgical tools he patented."

"I hope he took care of his children."

Egan took her hand and led her to the window. "See that illegally-parked beautiful red Porsche?"

" 'Nuf said." She smiled. "And you'd better get your ass down there PDQ!"

— Chapter 77 —
Two Weeks Later

CAS WAS NOT THRILLED about Hallie's appointment with the psychic, but his publisher had requested a personal pickup at the airport, and Cas could use the time alone with him. Hallie was delighted. Cas's disdain for "fortune tellers," along with his journalistic skepticism would be sensed by even a moderately intuitive woman.

Zlotta Kofiszny, "The World's Leading Celebrity

Psychic" lived and worked in a well-maintained Victorian house on Bush St., midway between uptown and downtown. No sandwich board with a giant hand or commercial sign indicated the occupation of its owner. The house number, however, was clearly visible under a dove of peace.

"Welcome, sister," said the man who answered the doorbell. "I'm Rev. Barney of the Church of Serenity. You are Miss Hallie?"

"Just Hallie." The Reverend, self-ordained she suspected, was short in stature, paunchy, and garbed in black — turtleneck, slacks, shoes. What little hair he had was combed across a bald pate. He reminded her of a smiley face.

"Madame Zlotta will be with you shortly. Please?" He gestured towards a brochure-covered desk. "Your donation to the church will be a hundred dollars for a thirty minute reading. If you wish the candle ceremony to protect you from negative energy, it's an extra eighty dollars."

"No candles," she said, "do you take credit cards?"

"Indeed we do. And we return your money if you're not satisfied."

Once paid, Rev. Barney pushed aside a pair of purple velvet draperies leading to a windowless room. A round table in the center held a single lit candle. The scent of incense was strong, the lights dim. Soft classical music played in the background.

Hallie took one of two chairs and glanced around. Painted walls echoed the magentas of the faded Persian carpet. An oversize portrait of a young Madame Zlotta dominated the room, her eyes seemingly fixed on the observer.

Gold-framed photos and clippings from various publications filled another wall. As Hallie was straining to read them, the psychic made a silent entrance.

She was not at all what Hallie expected. No gold loop earrings, no red bandana across her forehead, no long gypsy gown ending in Birkenstocks. Wrinkles, sparkling eyes and a bright smile adorned a once-pretty face framed by short white hair. Her wardrobe was in no way unusual. A flowery Gucci scarf topped a tailored tweed pantsuit. Black boots with laces completed the outfit.

Hallie jumped up. "I'm so sorry, I didn't hear you coming."

"Sit down, my child." She placed a hand on her arm. "As I thought. You're lovelier than the picture on your website."

"Thanks for telling me you checked it. Do you know why I'm here?"

"No," she replied, taking her chair, "and neither do you. The forces that brought us together are not known to either of us. If you can relax and stop judging me, I can tell you much about yourself."

"Actually, I was thinking how nice you look, and how well you speak English, with no accent. I'm wondering if you really do read kidney beans."

"I see you've done your homework, too. I can read kidney beans, tea leaves, coffee grains, tarot cards, corn husks, whatever picks up your vibrations. With each person it's different. But first, you have to trust and believe in what I do. And right now, in this room, only one of us is trusting."

Hallie smiled. The woman was not dumb. "I'm trying to keep an open mind. Are those tarot cards?"

"Indeed they are. I've read them for Paris Hilton, Ringo Starr and too many VIP's to name." She shuffled a deck of colored picture cards, set down nine and turned one over. "This is a mind-body spread based on your birthday. And I see a dark cloud of worry. Something heavy is weighing on your mind."

"You're right, Madame Zlotta, I do have concerns. I'm married to a journalist who doesn't believe in psychic powers, and I'm sort of a skeptic, myself. I do believe in people who are blessed with great sensitivity and intuition. And I'm sure you're one of them or you wouldn't have had such a successful career. But I really came to ask you —"

"I know why you *think* you came here. To ask about Dr. Frond."

"You are good!"

"And I will tell you what you want to know. Today we won't delve deeper. If you're as smart and perceptive as you seem, you'll come back to find out more about yourself. You'll want to learn how to protect yourself from negative energy…how to de-energize the mistakes in your past that haunt you…how to anticipate and create healthy barriers to thwart the jealousies and hostilities that envelop you."

"I know you honestly believe you can help me," Hallie said, "and I'm impressed by your openness. But right now my main concern is to find out what happened to Dr. Frond."

"That's easy, my child," she said quietly. "I killed him."

— Chapter 78 —

AN EERIE SILENCE filled the room. Hallie sat stunned, straining to understand. If Madame Zlotta was a murderer, why would she admit it? And if so, wouldn't she be dangerous? She found herself fervently wishing Cas were there.

"You seem surprised," said the psychic. "I pride myself on ridding the world of evil men and women. 'Be not envious of evil men, nor desire to be with them; for their hearts devise violence, and their lips talk of mischief.' Proverbs 24:1. Dr. Frond was evil and cruel, like Hitler, Stalin, Hirohito. I took care of all of them. Remember Ilse Koch, the 'Witch of Buchenwald'? Myra Hindley, the 'Moors Murderess,'? The world is better without them."

Hallie was beginning to understand. "How did you kill them?"

"The same way I killed Dr. Frond – with a deadly curse. Frydryk Czaplewski taught me the secret when I was nine years old in Poland. He was my music teacher. He knew I had psychic gifts even then. He made me promise to use my powers wisely, for spiritual healing, and never for personal reasons."

"Wasn't killing Dr. Frond personal?"

"No. He not only attacked me in his hateful book, he attacked my profession and everyone in it. I heard him give a radio interview and try to spread his malevolence. I couldn't let that go. It took me a year and a trip to Poland to gather the ingredients I needed to make the curse work. But I'm proud of what I did. I want the skeptics and naysayers of the world to know that the Lord gives us ways of dealing with our enemies. Does that answer your question?"

"Are you saying that you killed Dr. Frond from a distance? You never poisoned or touched him in any way?"

"There was no need. The worst poisons are intangible. Words have killed many more than daggers."

Hallie nodded. A glance at her wrist told her the half-hour wasn't quite up. "I won't tell anyone what you told me, Madame Zlotta. People might not understand. It's best we let his wife and children think he died of natural causes."

"As you wish. I can see that you're anxious to leave. I'd be happy to give you an extra half hour for a reading. No charge."

"That's very generous of you, but I have to get back to my office."

"No need to hurry. Darryl is most capable. And she's taking good care of that little boy in her tummy."

"A boy, is it?"

"He'll be healthy, but the poor dear will have a long labor. Hallie, my child, I know that you like to solve murders. All day, every day, thoughts from across the earth come to me in waves. My conscious mind sorts them out. What I can use, I keep. Feel free to come see me any time, if not for yourself, perhaps to help you fight the evil powers that threaten us all."

Hallie rose quickly and extended a hand. But Madame Zlotta's head was bowed, her eyes were closed and she was mumbling softly to herself. Hallie tiptoed out.

PART 12

— Chapter 79 —

MONDAY, APRIL SEVENTEENTH marked the three month anniversary of Edith Marsh's hip replacement, the beginning of Darryl's fourth month of pregnancy, and the first day of her catalog shoot. To celebrate her recovery, Mumsy invited her children to dinner, along with Darryl's parents, Stewart and Brenda Woods.

"You must be exhausted, my dear," Edith told Darryl, as they sat at the table. "How was your day?"

"I'm afraid it was exhausting. Posing for a catalog is a demanding process — so much to think about and remember."

Rob could hardly take his eyes off his beautiful wife. Pregnancy had softened her face in a most flattering way. "What was so tiring, honey?"

"We shot six different outfits. Standing still and posing is strenuous, yet you want to look glamorous, even with a big stomach. So while the makeup artist is curling your eyelashes with one hand and spraying your hair with the other, you try to wiggle yourself into a position the photographer likes. Then you have to hold it for another half hour while he fusses with his camera and lighting."

"It does sound exhausting," agreed Hallie.

Darryl laughed. "I forgot to mention that you're working for seven or eight hours, you're tired, you're thirsty, you have to go to the bathroom, and your feet are killing you, but you can't take off your shoes."

"Why in God's name do you do it?" asked Edith.

"Good question," said Rob.

Hallie jumped in. "Quit picking on her! It's her career. If she wants to continue modeling, she needs catalog shots in her résumé, and she'd be crazy not to do it."

"Darryl's career is going to be motherhood," offered her stepmother, who was usually too timid to speak.

"They're not mutually exclusive, Brenda," snapped Stewart Woods, giving his wife a look she understood. "And it's no one's business but hers."

"Would you like to hear about my visit to a psychic?" Hallie's save-the-day question turned all heads toward her. She held their interest and sparked a lively debate, until the butler, Grimaldi, entered with a cake lit with a single candle. He set it down in front of Darryl, who promptly placed it in front of Edith, saying, "Let's blow out the candle together." And they did.

"I'll have to pass on dessert," Stewart whispered to his host, who was already slicing into the cake.

Darryl overheard him. "But you love chocolate, Dad."

"Sorry, sweetheart. I've had too many carbs already."

"You're dieting? You look damn good to me, Stewart." Cas stood up. "May I offer a toast to our favorite mom-to-be, and to the best of all possible mothers-in-law? We're especially grateful that your pain is gone and you've regained your zest for life. Thank you for this happy celebration."

"Thank you," said a smiling Edith, raising her glass. "May God bless us all."

— Chapter 80 —

EARLY THE NEXT MORNING, Hallie was excited to hear from

173

Dr. Toy. After a brief apology for his absence, he informed her that, "I've emailed Dr. Frond's Autopsy Report to you, the police, his partner, and his wife."

"What did you find?" Hallie asked eagerly.

"Not a shred of evidence of foul play. The deceased had so many medical problems, I'm amazed he lived as long as he did. He had the heart of a ninety-year-old man. You can read about the rest."

"No poisons? Are you sure?"

"Nothing that wasn't self-inflicted. He had been injecting himself with testosterone cypionate, a powerful steroid. Did you know he was on steroids?"

"I just learned recently."

"If anyone killed Dr. Frond, it was Dr. Frond. The androgen warped his brain, must have warped his judgment. He had to be aware of the hyperhidrosis, gynecomastia —"

"English please?"

"Excessive sweating, enlarged breast tissue, strong body odors, weight gain, muscle gain, hair growth, and so on. Read the report. Out of respect for the family, the Death Certificate lists 'acute myocardial infarction' as the prime cause of death, with several underlying causes. There's every indication that the doctor took no steps to save his own life."

"Could you get in trouble for not calling it a suicide?"

"No, although another M.E. might disagree. A Death Certificate is always a matter of opinion. In my opinion, coronary artery disease was the culprit."

Hallie sat speechless, trying to fit all the pieces of the puzzle. "Where's Dr. Frond's body now?"

"In the cemetery."

"So that's it? That's all there is?"

"That's it for the Frond family. Absolutely no question that Dr. Frond died from health issues that he brought on himself, not only by the testosterone replacement therapy, but by neglecting to treat his heart condition. I believe that's the closure you've been waiting for."

He paused a moment, as if wondering whether or not to keep talking. Then he said, "It may be nothing, but I went over Kaycie Berringer's body again before I released it to her parents. I may have found something of interest. I'll get back to you."

Hallie was suddenly alert. "Really? What? When? Do you still have the body?"

"No, her parents had her cremated. But I have the evidence, if it is evidence. I'll know more in a week or two."

Later that morning, Hallie heard from Cas. "I just got a call from Dr. Frond's partner, Dr. Gilbert," he said. "Remember when I interviewed him and he promised to look for the results of Jerry Frond's medical tests?"

"Did he find them?"

"Yes. He knew about the steroid overdose when he put Jerry in the hospital, but he told Leah it was a virus. He said that had he been able to look at Jerry's EKG at the time, he'd have seen that his coronary arteries were seriously blocked by the buildup of plaque in the vessels. He would've tried to talk him into immediate surgery — even though he probably couldn't have convinced him. Jerry didn't trust other surgeons. He knew too much about what could go wrong. If he hadn't been so pigheaded, he might still be alive."

"Dr. Gilbert's words or yours?"

"His."

"I don't understand. Why did he call you?"

"He wanted to clear the air and explain that unless Dr. Frond's death had been ruled a homicide, he couldn't have broken doctor-patient privilege. He was sure it would all come out in the autopsy, and it did. So he was just glad it was over, and hoped I could influence Dr. Toy to do the right thing, that is, list the COD as cardiac arrest and play down the steroid poisoning."

"That's exactly what Dr. Toy did."

"I told him that. He sounded relieved."

"Then it's over," said Hallie, with a sigh. "Now Dr. Frond and his family can all rest in peace."

PART 13

— Chapter 81 —

WEDNESDAY MORNING at half past eight, Darryl Woods Marsh, as she'd started calling herself, was dressed, made-up, and sitting on a bench at Crissy Field, pretending to read a magazine. There were so many errands she could have done, she thought, if only she'd known the photographer was running late.

The day was ideal for pictures, warm, bright, and sparkling. But rather than sit and wait for the man with the camera, the stylist and the makeup man had gone strolling along the water, leaving Darryl alone with her musings.

Her mind went back to early December, and the wonderful walk she'd had there with Rob. Here she was, only four months later, not only married to the man, but soon to bear his child! It had all happened so fast, it seemed unreal. And although her friend Kaycie was gone, she'd found herself a new family. Hallie was the sister she never had, and Edith had actually begun showing some warmth.

Cas had welcomed Darryl to the clan, confiding, "We're the outlaws, not the in-laws." And she'd felt that way, too, in the beginning. Yet the other night when Cas toasted Edith's return to health, he'd sounded genuinely fond of her. Asked about it later, he admitted they had an unspoken truce, for Hallie's sake, and that Mumsy had given up trying to run their lives — almost.

Darryl had made a point of thanking her mother-in-law for including her parents in family gatherings. She knew it made her Dad happy to see her happy, and Rob had been so kind and attentive lately, she was thinking they really should be living together. She would mention it Friday when the catalog job was finished.

Thoughts of her Dad reminded her that he'd said something strange at dinner about not eating dessert and counting his carbs again. Why would he keep doing that if he didn't have a weight problem? Or did he? There was one way to find out.

The phone rang twice before Brenda answered. "Always good to hear from you, Darryl," she said. "How are you feeling?"

"Amazingly well, thanks."

"And how's our grandson?"

"You've decided it's a boy, have you? He does kick like one. But I was sort of a tomboy as a kid. How's Dad doing? Can you tell me about his health?"

"I'll let him tell you himself. He's right here and wants to talk to you."

Damn, she thought. She was hoping Brenda would fill her in when he wasn't around.

"Hi, sweetheart," came her father's warm voice. "Nothing wrong, I hope."

"What's your favorite expression? Snafu," she said, laughing. "I'm here at Crissy Field, all made up and waiting for the photographer. I was so glad to see you the other night, but I wondered about your not eating dessert. Are you having health problems?"

"All's well and under control. Tell me about you. How's the catalog coming along?"

"Dad," she said, exasperated. "Why do you always change the subject when I ask about your health? What aren't you telling me?"

"You're a worry wart, like your mother was." He quickly regretted bringing up his late wife. "Brenda takes great care of me. You'd be the first to know if either of us was seriously ill."

Good damage control, she thought. Brenda hated being compared with her predecessor. "Why are you still counting carbs?"

"Desserts aren't good for any of us. Speaking of food, can we get you and Rob here for dinner one night?"

"Oh, sure," she said, resigned to his attitude, "as soon as I finish the shoot."

"I'll remind Brenda to call you next week. Hope that thoughtless photographer shows up."

"Me, too, Dad. Love you. 'Bye."

— Chapter 82 —

ROB WAS RELIEVED when Friday came around — the last day of Darryl's catalog shoot. He had been driving her to work at different locations every morning, picking her up each evening, then reluctantly leaving her at her apartment and taking the elevator up to his own place. That ridiculous arrangement had to end. Strangely, they seemed to have grown closer living apart, and she had hinted that she felt as he did; they belonged together.

So far, the work had gone well for Darryl. Claude, the photographer, had told her the day before that he only needed her Friday morning; they would meet for some easy indoor shots and she could go home at noon.

Since she'd promised Rob he could watch her last

shoot, he parked his car in a South-of-Market garage, and together, they walked to the loft where Claude lived and worked. He was surprised and seemed somewhat annoyed to see Rob, but he shook hands, and yes, Rob could observe, as long as he stayed out of the way and didn't interrupt.

A large room with shade-covered windows served as a studio. Tall stands with both strobe and working lights supplied varying degrees of brightness. Against a wall, an open cabinet displayed an array of wigs, shawls, artificial flowers, hats, hair ornaments and various props. On a lower shelf, camera equipment shared space with assorted spot lights, reflectors, and rolls of background paper. Next to the cabinet stood a three-paneled screen; beside it hung a full-length mirror.

The stylist had brought Darryl a blue robe and matching slippers to model, helped her change behind the screen, then left for the day. The makeup artist finished Darryl's face and fluffed up her hair. Then he, too, was off for the weekend.

Rob sat quietly on a wooden chair, as far from the action as he could be. While Darryl was practicing poses in front of the mirror, he watched Claude's back as he adjusted his camera on a tripod. The man looked to be in his late forties, slightly overweight, with hunched shoulders. His face, mostly covered by dark stubble, had a tight, squinting expression. Although they'd just met a few minutes prior, something about him made Rob uncomfortable.

"We're good," Claude shouted. "Let's go!"

Standing before the white backdrop, Darryl began

swaying gracefully, following his directions to turn left, turn right, head up, head down, eyes here, eyes there — as he clicked away.

"You're uptight," he growled. "Relax, for God's sake. You're not in an evening gown, you're wearing a fucking bathrobe!" More directions, more clicks. With a loud sigh, he walked up, patted down her collar, and repositioned her arms.

Rob thought he saw Claude's hand "accidentally" brush her breast, but told himself he was overreacting.

Suddenly, the photographer changed tactics. "Ah, now you've got it, sweetheart, you look like a goddess, beautiful! Good, good, I love it! Spread your wings. That's it!" Click. "You've got it! Hold it there — look past my ear into the great beyond, ethereal, that's it — hint of a smile —now a bigger smile. You're happy. Your boyfriend's coming in the door. Big happy smile. Great!" Click, click.

Again, he walked up to her, tightened her sash and fussed with her neckline. "Too much cleavage, sweetie. Try standing straighter. That's it. Keep smiling!"

Although Rob could only see Claude's back, he was sure the guy was handling her far more than was necessary. And this time, his arm had definitely touched her breast. He wasn't imagining it. And what was that boyfriend crap?

"We're almost through, sweetie, we got some great ones. Now let's go for something different."

Rob watched the photographer deliberately place his hand on Darryl's buttocks as he swung her around. Her startled look told Rob all he needed to know. Jumping up from his chair, he rushed over, grabbed Claude's shirt collar, then landed a solid fist on his jaw.

Claude toppled backward, staring at Rob in shock. He clutched his chin in pain, groaned, and limped out of the room.

"Get dressed," Rob told Darryl.

She was in her clothes in three minutes. He took her arm as they hurried down the stairs to the exit. "I'm sorry, honey," he said, holding the door open for her, "It wasn't a hard punch. I didn't break his jaw. I know you'll probably never speak to me again, but that slimebag got what he deserved."

Darryl leaned forward and kissed his lips. "My big strong man came to my rescue," she said with a grin. "I love you more than ever."

— Chapter 83 —

AN EMAIL MESSAGE from the manager of ShowTime, the maternity shop, thanked Darryl for her week's work. The proofs were being Photoshopped, but they looked "excellent," and her check would go out in a few days.

Claude's name was not mentioned. Darryl was sure the photographer hadn't reported the punch to the jaw, since he already had a reputation for getting too friendly with the models. She hadn't ever been alone with Claude before, and Rob's presence, plus her pregnancy, had given her a false sense of security. Never again, she assured Rob, would she work with the creep — and undoubtedly, vice versa.

That evening, Darryl gave notice to the landlord,

and started the process of moving in with her husband.

The next three weeks, Darryl spent mornings helping Hallie at her office, and afternoons sorting through drawers and closets, filling several boxes with clothes and other possessions. On Saturdays, she and Rob distributed the goods to charities and thrift shops. They finally felt like the newlyweds they were.

PART 14

— Chapter 84 —

DARRYL'S LONG-AWAITED twenty-week date came in mid-May, when she could safely have a fetal ultrasound. The morning of her appointment, she told Rob, "I have to drink five glasses of water and not pee. The doctor said they can view the baby better if I have a full bladder."

"I'll pee for you," Rob offered, trying to hide his nervousness. What if something went wrong?

The procedure was to take half an hour and be painless. After Darryl changed into a gown at the University of California hospital's Vascular Lab, she lay on a padded bed, while the sonographer, a young Asian woman, rubbed her abdomen with a warm gel. Then the technician sat down at her keyboard. Rob stood behind her, watching the screen over her shoulder.

"This test doesn't use radiation," she explained, reaching to the bed and moving a small plastic "mouse" over Darryl's abdomen. "It uses high-frequency sound waves inaudible to the human ear. They're transmitted via this transducer, which looks inside the body and transforms the echoes into pictures of your baby."

At first a blur, followed by noises that sounded like a cat's meow, the picture soon came into focus. Rob grabbed Darryl's hand as he stared at the tiny fetus. "Is it — a girl?" he asked.

"A beautiful little girl," said the sonographer.

"Is she healthy?"

"The placenta looks just fine — very thin."

"What's that on top of her?" he wondered.

"That's another little girl. Congratulations! You're having twin daughters!"

186

Tears rolled down Darryl's face as Rob bent to kiss her. Too moved to speak, she simply squeezed her husband's hand.

— Chapter 85 —

ROB AND DARRYL were too keyed up to go home. Despite strong winds and cool May weather, they drove to Ocean Beach, parked outside the Cliff House, a landmark restaurant overlooking the Pacific, and strolled inside. While they waited for a table, Darryl excitedly called Hallie.

"Fabulous! Congratulations!" came the response. "Are they identical or fraternal?"

"We forgot to ask!"

"I'd knit you two pink blankets, if I knew how to knit." Hallie seemed thrilled. "I have news, too. Not as wonderful as yours, but I heard from Dr. Toy today. Remember when he told me he might have something of interest? Apparently, he went over Kaycie's angiomata — those little red bumps on her skin — and discovered that one of the bumps was used as — I think he called it a 'subcutaneous injection site.' Kaycie or someone else had injected her thigh in a spot where it wouldn't be noticed. Dr. Toy had to give her body to her parents for cremation, but he has the tissue sample and he's going to run tests."

"Will they tell him what was injected?"

"Doubtful, he said. He wanted me to ask you if you know any reason why Kaycie might have injected herself."

Darryl thought a moment. "She had allergies, especially to pollens. This time of year — spring — was always

187

hard for her. Her allergist wanted to give her desensitizing shots, but she didn't want to have to go to his office twice a week. He suggested she learn how to give herself the shots, but she said she hated needles and couldn't do it. So no, I can't buy the idea that she would ever inject herself."

"How strange. Dr. Toy said he could tell the site was recent. Could she have seen a doctor the morning of the day she died?"

"It's possible. I picked her up at ten-forty-five. Maybe her visitor was a doctor. But why would a doctor inject her in one of those red bumps? Why would a doctor inject her anyway?"

"Beats me." Hallie sounded puzzled. "I would've guessed medication, but Prozac and some sleeping pills were the only drugs in her bloodstream.

"We — Oops! Rob's telling me our table's ready, so we're going to have lunch. I could eat a moose."

"Better feed my nieces! I won't mention them to Mumsy. I'll leave that to you."

— Chapter 86 —

ON THEIR WAY to the Piedmont hills the next evening, Darryl and Rob stopped to share their good news with Edith. She was surprised and delighted, and insisted they start looking for a house which would be her gift — as long as they stayed in town and didn't live too far from her.

"She's trying to run things again," growled Rob, as they got back into their car.

"Are you kidding?" said Darryl. "She wants to buy

us a house and her only condition is that we live in the nicest part of the city. I couldn't believe her generosity!"

He smiled. "When you put it that way, I guess I shouldn't complain. All she has to do is sell one of her paintings. Then she could buy ten Gold Coast homes."

"She's being really good to us, Rob. Oh, here's where we turn left at the next stoplight."

Moments later, they parked outside the beige stucco house where Darryl grew up. A cherry blossom tree in full bloom brightened the front lawn. Colorful flowers lined both sides of the walkway. They were new additions, she noted, obviously planted by a professional. It seemed strange that Brenda was suddenly paying attention to the garden.

After the usual hugs, Brenda mentioned she'd invited two couples to meet "my new son-in-law." She seemed in unusually high spirits, and Darryl was amused to hear her talk about "Edith's art collection," and her dinners "in Edith's spectacular mansion."

Towards the end of the meal, Darryl quietly excused herself and headed for the bathroom. Along the way, she stopped to peek in her old bedroom. Seeing only her Dad's clothes in the closet, and a picture of herself on the dresser, she assumed that Brenda had taken over the master bed-room, and relegated her husband to the smaller room. Poor Dad, she thought.

Farther down the hall was the family room, which had barely changed. The big closet was still there; she wondered if it held the same light bulbs, tools, vacuum cleaners, all the practical things a home needs. A quick look confirmed that the shelves were packed with paper shopping bags, flashlights, cleaning utensils, and miscellaneous bric-a-brac.

A pile of linens seemed strangely out of place on the top shelf. Curious, she stood on tiptoes, pushed the stack aside, peered in closer, then gasped. The "hidden" object was a replica of a Tiffany table lamp with a stained glass shade. The dragonfly pattern was unmistakable. She had bought it as a gift for Kaycie when she first moved in with her.

Hurriedly replacing everything as she found it, she stopped in the bathroom, combed her hair and collected herself, then returned to the table. Rob was describing their ultrasound experience, saving the best part for Darryl.

"They want to know the baby's gender," he said proudly.

"Uh — we're having twin girls," she blurted. Her mind was still elsewhere, trying to make sense of what she'd seen.

Brenda was the first to cry out. "How wonderful — two little Marsh granddaughters for us! Darryl dear, you *must* give me a date for a baby shower."

The guests gave appreciative toasts. Stewart Woods got up to embrace his daughter, then patted Rob on the back. "Good work, son," he teased.

Rob grinned. "Aw, thanks, Dad. It was nothing."

Shortly after dessert, Darryl pleaded fatigue, accepted handshakes and hugs, and they left for home. Knowing Rob's aversion to anything having to do with Kaycie, she kept her surprising discovery to herself.

PART 15

— Chapter 87 —

SATURDAY MORNING, as soon as Rob left for a gig on the Peninsula, Darryl was on the phone to Hallie, relating what she'd found.

"Where'd you buy the lamp?" Hallie asked.

"There's a lighting store downtown, near my model agency. A few reproductions were on sale for a hundred and fifty bucks. That one caught my eye."

"What distinguished it from the others?"

"The dragonflies on the shade. Most of the others had designs and flowers."

"Hmmm. Did Brenda ever visit you at your flat?"

"Once she and Dad came for cocktails and we all — including Kaycie — went out for dinner. But that was months ago. And the lamp was still there in January when I moved out."

"But you've gone back to see Kaycie and get your things several times, haven't you?"

"Yes. I never told Rob I was seeing Kaycie. He'd have been furious. A few times I got lonely when he was off with his guitar somewhere, so I'd go visit her. We'd sit in the living room and watch TV, just like when I lived there. When the set was on, that lamp on the table by the couch was our only light. I would've noticed if it hadn't been there. Kaycie used to watch TV by it every evening."

"When you went to the flat the night Kaycie died, you said you didn't go in the living room."

Darryl nodded. "Correct."

"And when I went in there later, I asked you about the place on the table where something was removed. 'Something' must have been that lamp."

"Most likely."

They paused a few seconds to digest their thoughts. Then Darryl spoke first. "But how and when did Brenda get it? Kaycie loved it. She wouldn't have parted with it."

"Hold on, we don't even know for sure it's the same lamp. Suppose Brenda saw yours, liked it and bought one for herself?"

"Why would she hide it in a closet?"

"Maybe she was storing it. Maybe she didn't have room. That reminds me — would you have anything with Brenda's fingerprints on it?"

"I should've thought of that, but I didn't. How can we get them? How can we find out about the lamp?"

"I've an idea," said Hallie. "Tell you more on Monday."

— Chapter 88 —

THE FOLLOWING TUESDAY, the *Piedmont Daily News* ran a small color ad. A mature, elegantly-dressed woman was standing admiring a Tiffany desk lamp. The caption below the picture read:

Do you have a valuable table lamp hiding in an attic or tucked away in a closet? It may be worth more than you think!

Antique dealer Josh Caldwell recently sold this priceless Tiffany Lamp for $650,000. The buyer, a European collector, is offering top dollar for similar items.

Bring your Tiffany treasure(s) to the Anderson Caldwell Gallery this Saturday, May 21st, 1-5 p.m., for a free

appraisal. Please call for an appointment.
(Name, phone number, address, website)

Cas was not happy with Hallie's plan. "If you're going to carry out a sting," he told her that evening, when she showed him the ad, "you need a law officer there."

"It's not a sting," she protested. "If Brenda sees the ad and shows up with her lamp, she won't be committing a crime. There's no entrapment. We just want Josh to ask her where and how she got it."

"Josh is willing to do that?"

"Sure. He's a good friend. Mumsy's used him for appraisals and stuff for years. He sold the first painting of her collection, after Dad died, the one that launched her philanthropic career. I think it was a Degas."

"Did you tell him why you're curious about Brenda's lamp?"

"He didn't ask. He knows I like to solve crimes. Besides, maybe someone will turn up with a real Tiffany Lamp. He could make a fortune."

Cas shook his head in frustration. "Why can't you go on shopping sprees or organize ladies' luncheons or take the grandkids to the zoo like your friends do? Why do you have to get mixed up in murders? — especially when you don't even know if Kaycie's death was a murder."

"I don't go shopping because I have more clothes than I need, I hate to waste time at ladies' luncheons, and I don't have grandkids. Any more questions?"

"Why don't you have grandkids? You have to start with your own, you know. They don't come ready-made.

And you're thirty-five. You'll be over the hill in five years."

"Thanks for putting it so delicately." She giggled and cuddled up to him. "I'm willing to work on it if you are."

He grinned back. "Best offer I've had all day."

— Chapter 89 —

THE STING THAT WASN'T A STING, depending on one's definition, took place that Saturday at the private San Francisco antiques gallery. So as not to arouse suspicion, Hallie had run the ad in several Bay Area newspapers as well as in Piedmont.

The day before, Josh Caldwell had left her a message that, "The fish took the worm." His assistant, Ellen, later confirmed that she'd heard from Mrs. Stewart Woods of Piedmont, who would come by at 3:30 p.m.

The notice had attracted more than forty callers, many of whom wanted to know if they could bring in other treasures. Sorry, they were told, the gallery would be having more free-appraisal days, but this one was just for table lamps.

The appointments ran smoothly. A security guard checked names at the door, and Ellen sat at the table next to Josh, a concealed tape recorder on her lap.

Many of the items he examined were unworthy of an appraisal. People needed money in the depressed economy, and brought in whatever copies and reproductions they had. The project ended with no big finds but it had served its purpose.

Hallie and Darryl showed up at the gallery shortly after five.

"Thanks for everything," said Hallie, giving Josh a hug, "We're dying to hear the tape."

"She turned down a glass of water and didn't say much," he warned, "but she handled this paper so maybe you can get the fingerprints you wanted. Here's the tape. Sit down and listen."

Josh: That's a lovely piece, Mrs. Woods. Have you had it long?"

Brenda: "Quite a while."

Josh: You know it's a reproduction, of course. But it's one of the better ones. Where did you buy it?"

Brenda: It was a gift.

Josh: Do you know where the person who gave it to you bought it?

Brenda: No. I don't ask people who give me gifts where they got them.

Josh: I thought perhaps it came in a box or wrapping paper you might have recognized."

Brenda: Does it have any value?

Josh: That depends on its provenance. Would you be able to ask your friend where she bought it?

Brenda, sounding exasperated. "She's dead. Are you going to give me an appraisal?"

Josh: I need to know a little more. Are you online?

Brenda: Mr. Woods and I don't do computers. We have people who do it for us.

Josh: You're fortunate. You can buy reproductions

like this online for various prices. They sell for about two hundred dollars. (He hands her a paper with pictures and prices. She gives it a glance and hands it back.) However, yours is better than the average reproduction. The glass is high quality and I note it has Louis Comfort Tiffany's signature on the base.

Brenda: His real signature?

Josh: No, but as I said, this is an excellent copy. It doesn't merit an appraisal but I'd be willing to give you four hundred dollars for it right now. That's twice the online price, and no shipping charges."

Brenda: (After a pause) No thanks, it has sentimental value. Goodbye, Mr. Caldwell.

PART 16

— Chapter 90 —

DRIVING DARRYL BACK to her apartment building, Hallie stopped for a moment at the police station and dropped off the paper that, she hoped, had Brenda's prints on it. Along with that document, safely packed in plastic, she scribbled a note to Detective T. Baer, asking if he could match the prints to the Splenda wrapper and faucet prints in Kaycie Berringer's evidence envelope. She looked forward to hearing from him.

"Our brilliant sting didn't prove much," said Darryl, once Hallie was back at the wheel.

"On the contrary. It proved Brenda was reluctant to talk about the lamp, that the person she got it from was dead, and that she wouldn't take four hundred bucks for something that was worth — at the most — two hundred. I think she may have suspected something. She wasn't about to leave Josh the stolen evidence."

"I wonder...." Darryl was pensive a few moments. Then she asked, "Suppose the prints match. What will that prove?"

"The tea bag I found was still wet, so someone was definitely there. If Brenda's prints match those on the Splenda envelope, it will tell us that she was in Kaycie's flat early that morning. It will tell us that Brenda stole the lamp and stashed it in her car, most likely when Kaycie wasn't paying attention. You said she was seriously drowsy when you picked her up."

"It's weird," said Darryl. "Brenda hardly knew Kaycie. Why would she be visiting her? And what motive could she have for harming her?"

"We don't know that she harmed her. Let's sleep on

it, Darryl, and don't tell Rob anything. I'll phone you as soon as I hear from TB."

— Chapter 91 —

THE CALL CAME SOONER than expected. No doubt about the lab results, the detective said. Brenda's prints matched those on the wrapper. TB offered to bring the woman in for questioning, but Hallie asked him to wait. They still had nothing to connect her with Kaycie's death.

While she was mulling over what to do, another call came in, this one from Brenda. "Hallie, dear, we must have a baby shower for Darryl. Would you be interested in co-hosting with me?"

"What a lovely idea, Brenda — though I'm afraid my apartment's too small. Perhaps we can get a private room in a restaurant. Leandro's would be perfect. Shall I look into it?"

"I've never been there. Let's have lunch and check out the room. How does Wednesday look?"

"Fine. I'll make a reservation — noon?"

"Wonderful, Hallie. I have your address. I'll come by and pick you up."

"Terrific. See you then."

In Hallie's office the next morning, Darryl was disturbed to hear about the lunch date. "Our little Tiffany Lamp plan may have backfired," she told Hallie, dropping the mail on her desk. "Suppose she's on to you? She knows you've been trying to find out what happened to Kaycie. Suppose she did kill Kaycie and decides to kill you, too."

"You don't care much for your stepmother, right?"

"I've never liked Brenda. I think she loves Dad, though, and I know he needs her to take care of him. He finally broke down and told me he has juvenile diabetes – he's apparently had it for ages. But he says it's under control and he could live for years."

Hallie's eyes widened as she stared in disbelief. Then she slapped her forehead. "Oh, my God," she whispered, "That's the answer! That's it!"

— Chapter 92 —

LEANDRO'S WAS A SMALL, elegant restaurant in Presidio Heights. Power-women liked it because the food and service were excellent, the portions not too large, the booths offered a certain amount of privacy, the lights were low and flattering, and perhaps most important, they had valet parking. The room in the back, not too creatively called "The Back Room," was a popular spot for luncheons, meetings, and events that called for a long table seating thirty.

Shortly after noon on Wednesday, Hallie entered the restaurant with Brenda, and gave the hostess her name. They were shown to a booth.

"Shall we take a quick look at The Back Room?" Hallie asked.

"Let's eat first," said Brenda. "It smells good and I'm hungry."

A bespectacled waitress named Sara rattled off the specials. "The carrot soup is excellent and very healthful," she added, "and the halibut is fresh."

"Sounds good," said Hallie.

"Not to me." Brenda closed her menu and handed it to Sara. "I'll have the Salade Niçoise, dressing on the side, and two cups of hot water. I brought some rose blossom tea for us."

Hallie nodded approvingly. "I'll have what she's having."

"That's easy, I don't even have to write it down," said Sara, writing it down. "Two Salades Niçoise, dressing on the side, two cups of tea without the tea."

Then she disappeared.

The women chatted about nothing in particular, until Brenda asked, "How are you coming with your investigations?"

"We're doing fine. We know Dr. Frond's death was virtually a suicide because he neglected all the warning signs of a heart attack. Plus, he was injecting himself with a potent steroid. The M.E. called it coronary artery disease to save face for the family."

"Nice of him. And Kaycie?"

"We're still working on it. We tend to think her death wasn't a suicide. We traced the man who was sending her threatening letters, but that went nowhere. We haven't eliminated her father, George Berringer, as a suspect. Some new clues turned up recently."

"What new clues?"

"The crime lab's working on them," Hallie said casually. "We think Kaycie may have had a visitor that morning, before Darryl picked her up for the brunch. We'll see what the lab turns up."

Brenda shook her head. "Doesn't sound right to me. From what Darryl said, Kaycie was a loner with serious mental problems. She didn't have any friends, except for Darryl. That's why she felt her life was over when Darryl got married. She had no reason to go on living."

"We're open to all possibilities."

"Have you questioned their landlord? Darryl told me they had a crazy woman living next door."

"Oh, yes," Hallie laughed. "I've met Madame Goshenka. I don't think she's clever enough to kill someone and make it look like suicide. Sooner or later, we'll get to the bottom of this."

"I'm sure you will," smiled Brenda, reaching into her purse. She brought out two tea bags. "Take one. It's wonderful tea — relaxing and soothing."

"How thoughtful of you!" Hallie plucked a tea bag and dropped it into the cup of hot water Sara had just set down. She noticed Brenda laid the other tea bag on the side of her cup. When she looked a moment later, a tea bag was in the water.

Brenda stirred the brew. "It needs to steep for a while."

"Maybe we could check the Back Room before our lunch gets here?"

"Our food will be coming soon."

"Let's go look, anyway. We'll be right back," Hallie told the waitress.

— Chapter 93 —

SOMEWHAT RELUCTANTLY, Brenda followed Hallie to the rear of the restaurant. The Back Room was a spacious area, decorated with historic pictures of old San Francisco and its characters.

"That's Emperor Norton," Hallie pointed out. "He was a self-proclaimed Emperor, one of our first homeless street persons. And that's Lillie Hitchcock Coit, who loved to smoke cigars, dress like a man, and chase fires. And look, here are the Big Four, the railroad barons who —"

"I failed history in high school," Brenda interrupted. "I don't give a rat's ass about the past. It's like that dumb genealogy Stewart seems to find so fascinating. Who cares what our ancestors did or who they were? We can't take credit or blame for what they did. It has nothing to do with our lives now."

"You've a point, Brenda. I guess we all have our own interests. What are yours?"

"I just take care of my husband. This room looks fine. Let's get back to our table."

"But wait. We need to figure out how many we're inviting and where Darryl will sit to open her gifts."

"Gifts?"

"It's a shower, remember? We need a theme, too. We can't just say it's a baby shower."

"I've seen the room. That's enough for me."

"You *are* hungry," said Hallie, letting her lead the way back to their booth.

— Chapter 94 —

AFTER FINISHING THEIR TEA AND SALADS, Brenda asked if Hallie had any interest in seeing the current exhibit at the Legion of Honor Museum.

"I'd love to go," Hallie answered, scratching her forehead, "but for some reason, I'm feeling awfully sleepy. I took a hay fever pill this morning and I'm afraid it's catching up with me."

"The fresh air will revive you. Let's take a drive and see how you feel."

"Don't think I'm up to it, Brenda." Hallie covered a yawn. "Perhaps you should drop me at home…"

"You'll feel better once we get out of here. It's hot, and too crowded for my taste." She motioned to Sara for the bill.

"We — must — split the check."

"I can see you're not feeling well, Hallie." Brenda waved her credit card and Sara quickly took it. "You can get it next time."

"Wow — I'm not even sure I can — walk…"

"Of course you can. I'll help."

Hallie struggled to stand while Brenda signed the check, then took her guest's arm. Once out the door, she gave her ticket to the valet. Moments later, he brought her car.

"The lady seems ill," he said, staring at Hallie, who seemed to have trouble keeping her footing. "Should we call an ambulance?"

"No, thanks, she'll be fine. Just help me get her in

the car, please."

"Sure thing. I'll strap her in, too."

Soon they were headed toward the Museum, driving a wooded road along steep cliffs overlooking the ocean. Unexpectedly, Brenda pulled over and stopped the car.

"You don't fool me, Miss Hallie. The drug don't act that fast. You're faking it!" Brenda slapped her hard in the face.

Hallie didn't react. Her head simply rolled to the other side.

Brenda tried again, socking a fist into her eye. Still no reaction. "Well, I'll be damned. You're really out of it."

Losing no time, she reached into the glove compartment, brought out a syringe, and filled it from a small vial of colorless liquid. "Now to find a spot," she mumbled, patting Hallie's body. "Goddamn leather pantsuit!"

Rather than waste precious seconds trying to undo her jacket, Brenda reached up and opened Hallie's mouth. As she raised the needle, Hallie's right hand suddenly whipped around, grabbed her fingers and squeezed hard, forcing her to release the syringe. Snatching it with her other hand, she stabbed it into Brenda's thigh and pushed the plunger.

Brenda screamed.

"Scream all you want," said Hallie, wide awake and alert. "I assume that's fast-acting insulin and that you'll be dead shortly unless I give you something to counteract it."

Pale with fear, Brenda cried, "I need sugar! Hurry! Hurry!"

"Not so fast, dear friend. Did you kill Kaycie?"

"No! No! Please! I need sugar!"

"And I need a confession. Did you kill Kaycie?"

"Yes! Yes, I killed the stupid bitch! Now give me the sugar!"

"Did you just try to kill me?"

"Yes! Yes, I tried to kill you! PLEASE!"

"Hold out your hands."

Hallie grabbed a pair of handcuffs from her purse and locked Brenda's wrists. Then she tore open a breakfast-size packet of honey and emptied it on Brenda's tongue. "That'll hold you till the ambulance comes, but not much longer."

A quick call assured her both the police and the ambulance were on their way. It was time to turn off her tape recorder.

PART 17

— Chapter 95 —

Two days later, Officer Theodore "TB" Baer sat in one of the stark interrogation rooms at police headquarters. His partner, Fred Kowalski, preferred to stand. Seated opposite them, Brenda Woods, in a two-piece orange jail suit, had again been given her rights. Behind the one-way window, Hallie, her left eye covered with a bandage, watched the questioning with Cas and police Lieutenant Kaiser.

"You know you have the right to have a lawyer present," said TB, after introducing himself and Fred.

Brenda spoke slowly. "I can't afford one, and my husband won't pay for one. He wants me in prison so he can divorce me and screw around with all his women."

"If you can't afford a lawyer, we can supply one."

"I don't need a friggin' lawyer! You want the truth, right? And the truth will show that I'm innocent."

TB passed her a paper. "Then sign this release, please. It says that you understand your rights."

She scribbled her name and handed it back.

"Thank you. Let's start at the beginning, Brenda. You seem to have recovered from your unfortunate experience. I'm glad you got to the hospital in time. We have you on Ms. Marsh's tape recorder confessing to the murder of Kaycie Berringer."

"What would you say if someone held a gun to your head? Your sweet little Ms. Marsh had just injected me with the fast-acting insulin I carry around for my husband. I knew I desperately needed some form of sugar to counteract the insulin. It was either my life, or confessing to something I didn't do."

"Tell us about it."

"Kaycie Berringer was crazy, you know?" She tapped her head. "Really nuts. I knew she had a gun because she'd tried to kill my stepdaughter Darryl's boyfriend once — before they got married. So yeah, I went to see Kaycie that morning before the brunch. She had a Tiffany lamp of mine I wanted to pick up. But then she started talking about Darryl's babies as her babies, and how she didn't care about the father. Said she was going to court to get joint custody of the baby. She'd testify that she and Darryl were lovers and Darryl had purposely gotten pregnant so they could have a baby. She said she'd spend every cent she had and the rest of her life fighting for that baby!"

"Go on."

Brenda took a gulp of water. "I knew Kaycie would make nothing but trouble for Darryl and her new family — my new family, too. What would Edith Marsh think if Kaycie told them that her and Darryl had been lovers?"

"Is that true?"

Brenda shrugged. "Yeah, but then Darryl met Rob and she liked the idea of marrying a rich guy so she dumped Kaycie, and Kaycie was mad. She told me she was going to the brunch to make trouble."

"You wanted to stop Kaycie and spare your step-daughter Darryl the pain and embarrassment. I can under-stand that," said TB, in a kind voice. "You were trying to help."

"Exactly! I'd just come from the drug store and I'd picked up my sleeping pills and my husband's medication. I thought if I could slip a few of my tiny pink pills into her coffee mug, she'd be too tired to go."

"That was the Ambien they found in the autopsy. You were being thoughtful."

"Exactly!" she repeated. "So after awhile, Kaycie nodded off in her chair. I was scared she'd wake up in time to go to the brunch, so I thought I'd give her a light dose of my husband's insulin."

"How much did you give her?"

She shrugged. "I didn't measure. I injected her, washed our mugs and put them away, but I was in a hurry and I guess I left my sweetener wrap and tea bag in the sink. You found them and got my prints and that's how come you knew I was there, right?"

"Pretty much," said TB, still sounding sympathetic. "Let's see if I have this right. You left the house assuming you'd given Kaycie just enough insulin to temporarily put her to sleep so she wouldn't be able to go to the brunch."

"I thought I was doing the right thing — for my husband, Stewart, for my stepdaughter, Darryl, and for our unborn grandchildren. When I left, Kaycie was alive and sleeping. I picked Stew up at the hotel and we drove home. On the way, he told me that his new medication was delayed release insulin. I got real scared that it wouldn't affect Kaycie in time, and she might still go to the brunch and screw up Darryl's marriage. But there was nothing more I could do."

"Did it occur to you to call someone and get help for her?" asked Detective Kowalski.

"I didn't think she needed help. I didn't know she'd taken all that Prozac and wanted to off herself. Her own medicine killed her! I'm just a housewife. I'm no friggin'

211

murderer and you can't prove otherwise!"

A knock on the door summoned TB outside. He excused himself.

— Chapter 96 —

"SHE'S LYING!" EXCLAIMED HALLIE, as soon as the interrogation room door closed. "Every word out of her foul mouth is a lie!"

"Calm down, honey," said Cas, putting his arm around her.

Lieutenant Helen Kaiser turned to the detective. "I'm going to have to go, and Hallie and Cas can't stay here without me. But keep questioning, TB, you're doing fine. She seems to like you."

"I'm a nice guy," he smiled. "And I can lie, too."

"We've got her on video, see if she'll write out her story and sign her statement. Get her a public defender, whether she likes it or not. Hallie and Cas, you'll find Darryl and Rob and Mr. Woods down the hall, waiting to hear what's happening. TB will join all of you as soon as the interview's over. It may take an hour or so. Have some coffee and relax."

"Thanks for everything, Helen." Cas gave her a hug.

"You've been great," echoed Hallie, embracing her. "Of all my husband's ex-girlfriends, you're the best."

The Lieutenant laughed. "Considering the size of the list, that's quite a compliment."

Chapter 97

AN HOUR AND A HALF LATER, Detectives TB and Kowalski joined Hallie, Cas, Rob, Darryl, and her father, Stewart Woods, in a separate room. TB pressed a remote on the table and pointed to a TV screen. "Let's watch a video of our interview with Brenda Woods. Please save your comments till it's over."

"Will you record our rebuttal?" asked Hallie.

"Yes, and the D.A. gets the whole package. Here goes…"

As soon as the video ended, TB turned on his tape recorder. "Now it's your turn, Hallie," he said, after stating time, date, and the names of those present. "What's your reaction to the interview with Mrs. Brenda Woods?"

"Thanks, Detective," Hallie began, "I'll try to keep this brief. First, Brenda Woods did not visit Kaycie to pick up her Tiffany lamp. It wasn't hers; it was a gift to Kaycie. Apparently Brenda thought it was valuable enough to steal, because she obviously did so when Kaycie was knocked out, the morning of the brunch. Darryl has since seen it at Brenda's house."

"Why *did* Brenda go see Kaycie?" asked TB.

"I think she'd heard that Kaycie was upset and depressed about Darryl's leaving. She knew that Kaycie was furious that Darryl was depriving her of 'their' babies. If Kaycie went public with her claims, it would not only embarrass Darryl and Rob, it would threaten Brenda's new relationship with the Marsh family, which she treasured more than gold. She dropped the Marsh name every chance she got."

"It was — an obsession," added Stewart Woods. "Brenda thought Darryl's marriage and the twin grandchildren would be her membership card to San Francisco society. She talked of moving to the city and buying a condo on Nob Hill. She had big plans — and Kaycie threatened those plans."

"Unfortunately," Hallie went on, "Darryl had told Kaycie she loved her as a friend, so Kaycie believed they were lovers in all senses of the words."

"Brenda said they *were* lovers," reminded Detective Kowalski.

"No way!" exclaimed Darryl.

Hallie put her finger to her lips. "As soon as I heard that Mr. Woods, Brenda's husband, was diabetic, I called Dr. Thomas Toy of the San Francisco County Coroner's office, who'd done the autopsy. I asked if he'd tested the blood for insulin, and he said it wasn't included in the usual tox screen. He promptly tested a blood sample and found a high level of Humilin N or NPH insulin, which has an onset of one to two hours, and peaks at four to ten hours, about the time Kaycie died. Dr. Toy said he would change the Cause of Death to 'Acute Insulin Poisoning.' "

"That doesn't prove that Kaycie and Darryl weren't lovers."

"No, Detective, but the original autopsy showed that Kaycie's genitals were intact. She was a virgin."

"That still doesn't prove anything."

"My wife is *not* bisexual and never was," insisted

Rob, restraining his annoyance.

TB nodded to show he'd heard the protest. "Do you believe Mrs. Woods didn't realize she was injecting a lethal dose?"

"Not for a second," Hallie replied.

"May I speak?" asked Stewart Woods. He didn't wait for an answer. "Brenda's been taking care of me and my Type 1 diabetes since the day we got married five years ago."

All eyes turned to him.

"Most people are Type 2 diabetics," he continued. "They can usually get by with changes in diet and lifestyle. But Type 1 diabetics depend on daily insulin injections for survival. And Brenda's a jealous, possessive woman. She learned all she could about the disease and purposely made me dependent on her for my shots. She'd test my blood sugar, carefully measure every unit of insulin, and knew exactly what she was doing. I often wondered how I'd let her take control of my life, but it was easier that way, and I was lazy. She —"

"Bottom line, Stewart?" asked Hallie.

"My point is that Brenda had to know exactly what she was doing when she injected Kaycie with delayed release insulin. She also must have known that the insulin she used to try to kill Hallie was quick acting."

"Thanks for clarifying, Dad," said Darryl.

"You see, Mr. Detective," Stewart went on, "for an insulin-dependent diabetic, the body doesn't automatically correct our sugar levels, so we have to do it ourselves. If we don't, our blood sugar level starts to drop, and we can slip into a diabetic coma and die. That's why —"

The ring of TB's cell phone interrupted. "Let's take a ten-minute break," he said, turning off the recorder and hurrying out the door. His partner followed.

PART 18

— Chapter 98 —

THE TEN MINUTE BREAK turned out to be almost an hour break, with TB apologizing and explaining that a missing child's body had been found. He'd had to do the hardest part of his job: tell the parents.

"We shouldn't need much more of your time," he told Hallie, as he clicked on the recorder. "Suppose you tell us what happened in the restaurant. As you heard, Brenda denied that she tried to drug your tea, and said she was simply driving you to an art exhibit when you turned on her."

'Oh boy," said Hallie, shaking her head. "She should write fiction. Well, as you know, we went to Leandro's. By that time, I was pretty sure she was our killer and I dropped some hints that we were waiting for fingerprints and were hot on the trail of a suspect. I also knew the hostess at Leandro's, who agreed to pretend she didn't know me, and greeted me like a stranger. She'd helped me arrange to have my best friend, Sara Redington, disguise herself with thick glasses so none of the customers would recognize her, and pretend to be our waitress."

"Sara and I had arranged signals," Hallie went on. "Just before Brenda and I left to check the back room, I touched my tea cup and Sara got the message. Fortunately, the restaurant had the same kind of rose blossom tea — it's sort of a new 'in' fad. As soon as we were out of sight, Sara exchanged the tea made with Brenda's tea bag for a new brew made with the restaurant's tea bag, which I drank. The rose blossom tea was pink and so was the Ambien, so Brenda didn't notice any color difference. Sara saved the evidence and I'm sure the crime lab will prove my story."

"It already has," said TB. "Brenda's tea bag was

infused with approximately 20 milligrams of zolpidem tartrate — Ambien."

Hallie nodded. "I was pretty sure it would be. I pretended to be sleepy, then unconscious. That's when Brenda slapped me and punched me in the face. It hurt like hell but I knew if I reacted, I'd be dead. I got a black eye and some bad bruises, but it won't affect my sight."

"You were damn lucky!" Cas exclaimed. "If I'd known what you were up to..."

"Sorry, darling, I was foolish. I knew it was risky. I'd worn my leather pantsuit in case she tried to inject me. That protected my body, but she was going for my mouth. She figured a puncture site under the tongue might never be found. My eyes looked closed but they were open just enough so that I could see her hand coming up at me. That's when I grabbed the needle and jabbed her. I'd brought along some honey in case I might need it, and you know the rest. She needed it, and I wouldn't give it to her till she confessed."

"She got away with murder-by-insulin once, so she assumed she could do it again," said Darryl. "Where'd you get the handcuffs?"

"I've had 'em for awhile. Bought 'em online."

"Are we through?" Rob inquired. "I'd like to take my wife home."

"For the moment," said TB. "Thanks for your help. Any questions?"

"Can we keep this out of the media?" asked Hallie.

"You can try. You must have good contacts — I suggest you use them."

"One more question," said Stewart, with a sigh. "Anyone know a good divorce lawyer?"

— Chapter 99 —
Five Days Later

ALL EDITH MARSH wanted for her 60th birthday on June 1st, was a quiet dinner with her family. Surrounded by Hallie, Cas, Darryl, Rob, and Stewart Woods, she sat at the head of her table and offered a toast.

"To Darryl and Rob, soon to be parents, to my beautiful twin granddaughters-to-be, and my dear friend Stewart, thank you for helping me celebrate this occasion. Here's to all of us, to all who are not as blessed as we, and to Hallie and Cas, whose offer on a new house was just accepted. Congratulations and God willing," she smiled, tipping her glass to her daughter, "you'll soon fill it with the sound of little feet."

"Mother!" cried Hallie.

"I'm willing," said a delighted Cas, as all sipped their wine.

"Fifty percent is better than nothing," said Edith. "And Cas, please go through her shoe closet and give away those stilettos so she doesn't take another spill. That's a nasty black eye she got."

"I agree. Maybe one of these days she'll listen to us."

"I was sorry to hear about Brenda," added Edith, turning to Stewart. "Hallie told me she was involved in Katy's death and she's in jail. How terrible for you."

"Kaycie, Mom, not Katy," said Rob.

"Stewart raised his glass. "Here's to you, Edith, and thanks for caring. I'm sorry to say Brenda's seriously sick and I've started divorce proceedings. She's not the woman I married."

"They say some divorces are made in heaven," offered Rob. "Not mine, of course."

"Good recovery," said Darryl, poking him with her elbow.

Talk continued through dinner until Rob introduced a new subject. "The last time I invited you all to hear me play didn't turn out too well, I'm sorry to say."

"That's an understatement," murmured Hallie.

He went on: "I've a new invitation for all of you and you'll be glad to hear it's not a brunch. My quartet and some other musicians will be donating our talents to an evening concert at the Yerba Buena Center for the Arts. It's for a great cause and I'd like you all to buy my most expensive tickets."

"What's the cause?" asked Hallie. "A new guitar for you?"

"Whatever the date we'll be out of town," said Cas.

"Thanks a lot, guys. Umm — it's sometime in June and I'll let you know. It's a benefit for the new SFJAZZ Center that's going up at Fell and Franklin Streets. It'll be the first stand-alone three-story jazz venue in the country!"

Hallie winced. "People are homeless and hungry and you're building a music hall? Sounds like Nero fiddling while Rome burned."

"Not at all. It'll be a fantastic neighborhood gathering place where kids can have fun listening to good music, go to classes, and learn to play instruments instead of selling dope on the streets."

"Of course we'll buy tickets, Rob dear," said Edith. "It sounds like a most deserving cause. I suppose I can dig up someone to go with me."

"Umm-harrumph." Stewart cleared his throat. "Hope you don't think I'm being too presumptive, Edith, but if you wouldn't mind the company of an elderly soon-to-be-bachelor, it would be my greatest pleasure to buy our tickets and escort you."

"Why, Stewart!" Edith's face lit up. "How very kind of you! I — I don't know what to say."

"How about 'Yes'?"

"Well, then, yes, thank you. I'd love to have a handsome escort, if you don't mind spending an evening with a sexagenarian."

"I don't know about the sex part," he said, laughing. "But I think I can handle everything else."

— **Chapter 100** —

DRIVING HOME, Cas couldn't wait to chat. "Let's see," he said, "If Edith marries Stewart, Darryl's twins will have a step-grandfather and a grandfather-in-law, only they'll both be the same man."

"That's absurd," said Hallie. "Why would Edith want to get married? And why would Stewart? He's an attractive man and there aren't many single guys around for older women. He'll be fighting them off."

"How old is he?"

"Darryl says he's sixty-one."

"Guys in their sixties usually like gals in their forties or younger. And Stewart seems to like gals of any age."

"When I'm sixty," Hallie noted, "you'll be sixty-four. Will you trade me in for a younger model?"

"Possibly. Especially if you continue to go snooping into other people's murders."

"Who — me? Darling, seriously, wouldn't it be nice if Stewart married Mumsy and got her out of our hair?"

"You're changing the subject. What about poor Stewart's hair? — what's left of it."

"He's used to a strong, dominating woman."

"Well, I'm not. So you'd better shape up and start behaving yourself."

"When I'm bad I'm very good," she said, nestling up to him and nibbling his ear. "Do I still have to behave myself?"

"Yes," he whispered, pulling her closer, "starting tomorrow."

***

CPSIA information can be obtained at www.ICGtesting.com
Printed in the USA
BVOW021048270112

281332BV00001B/8/P

9 780915 090396